RAIN DROPS AND CATERPILLARS

Anuradha Prasad

ISBN 978-93-52011-48-3
Copyright © Anuradha Prasad, 2019

First published in India in 2019 by Inkstate Books
An imprint of Leadstart Publishing Pvt. Ltd.

Sales Office:
Unit No. 25-26, Building No. A/1,
Near Wadala RTO,
Wadala (East), Mumbai – 400037, India
Phone: +91 96 99933000
Email: info@leadstartcorp.com
www.leadstartcorp.com

Disclaimer: The views expressed in this book are those of the author and do not necessarily reflect the opinion of the Publisher.

Editor: Vikrant Bharadwaj
Cover: Dhiraj Navlakhe
Layouts: Victor patali

Forward

Transformation is sometimes ....like - surviving a war!

Dedication

Hope, dream and looking forward— is life!

This book is an allegiance to those people, who have made very small changes without realizing the magnanimity of the paradigm shift they made for others. To those too, who are standing at the helm!

Those unknown faces, those real people who, mirrored my stories!

About the Author

Anuradha Prasad is an artist, speaker and an author. She has worked with and published thousands of articles for top newspapers and magazines . She has a PhD. in English literature from Mumbai University and was on the cover of Times' 'West Side Plus' and several notable publications.

'Two Winters and 365 Days' and 'Coming Back Home' were her previous books.

'Rain Drops and Caterpillars' is her third.

She often deals with self-discovery and internal transformation of the characters in her writings.

While the 'The Statesman', 'News Today' and the 'Pioneer' listed her books as outstanding on their shelves, the newspapers like, Dainik Jagran, Panjab Kesari, Story Zen have described her as a writer with a realistic edge, capable of stirring deep emotions in a reader. Kindle edition of 'Coming Back Home' exceeded 10,000 downloads early this year.

Blogging, observing nature, traveling, listening to music and watching Bollywood movies are her many passions.

https://www.facebook.com/
AuthorAnuradhaPrasad/

https://mobile.twitter.com/anuradhap2?lang=en

website- www.anuradha-prasad.com

Acknowledgements

To the people who let me be when I am banging away at the keyboard, that does not stop till I complete a manuscript, I envisioned! They are my closest under the roof buddies! - My family! The first in the hierarchy as I famously put it is- 'The love of my life - My husband!'

Secondly, the apple of my eyes. The young lady in the house, who does not mince words if required to criticize or to praise is- my daughter. Thank you always for your honest opinions!

Friends, enemies, frenemies in that order. Friends for being concerned about the outcome. Enemies suffering from what I call en-vicity! Frenemies for mixed reactions!

Naina and Vikrant for walking all the steps with me till the completion to Publishing.

A Special mention - Dhiraj for creating that 'One in a million cover' and for keeping patience till he reached that perfect image. All the readers and well-wishers. Thanks a million!

Sublimity

Roushni wore the head phones and looked through the glass partition. The two guys outside the partition put their head phones too. She looked at them expectantly. She stood there with her hands crossed on to her chest. It was a gesture that told the outsiders that she was ready but not started yet. She would, when the signal goes up!

One guy was in his mid-forties while the other one was in his early twenties his assistant. Both men on the other side of the glass were working animatedly. There was pin drop silence in the place. They were working on the click board, setting the base track. It started!

Roushni felt the sound. The vibration from it was moving the very floor she was standing on. Her body started to move a bit as her nerves sensed the tune.

After the two men decided on the tempo, they set the guide rhythm, a simple drum sequence to the tune. Both looked at each other and nodded in approval.

Roushni felt the vibrations change from her side. Now she felt the intense bass tremors through her ears into her body that travelled right to the tip of her toes. She recognized it as a percussion that was now added to the base instrument. Her right foot caught the timing and started to thump. Her heart beat added to the tempo. Her entire being felt alive!

She waited with bated breath, hands crossed on her side. She felt new and alive. As every time felt like the first time to her!

Except for the lights on the instruments and the cubicle the studio was drenched in darkness and the sounds did not escape from the soundproof room either. It was a no-entry zone!

The two people in the darkness from their corner looked on quietly. The shadows doused over the floor from them, moved when they did.

Except for a lone movement nothing was visible. In the shadows they sat earnestly soaking in the sounds hand-in-hand, as feelings and emotions passed through them back and forth!

The sound recordist and the senior music director finally set the base track and the guide rhythm to their satisfaction and gave a thumbs up. The singer reciprocated.

The director went on signaling throughout the recording. He looked like a traffic police man, maneuvering every bit of the moving traffic. The singer never took her eyes off him! She worked her song through the gaps in the music, through the highs and lows as they had practiced earlier. Finally, the music stopped as the gawky director stood up and crossed his chest this time to signal the end. Roushni lifted her open palm to signal the end and removed the headphones so did the other two on the other side. The figures emerged from the shadows hand-in-hand.

Roushni came out of the cubicle. The director shook hands while the assistant looked on admiringly. The old couple stood at a respectable distance for some time before the lady stepped forward and hugged her.

"You did great Roushniji!" said the admiring man. The assistant nodded in agreement.

Roushni smiled more broadly. She signaled a thank you along in a low note, "Thank you." It was an usual prolonged one with a broad smile. She looked beautiful.

"Thank you! Ma. Thank you! Pa"

"It is our pleasure!" The couple chanted together like an anthem!

The small group came out from the studios after a while and walked out in different directions after exchanging pleasantries.

The couple along with Roushni walked to the car parked out. They all sat while the vehicle sped homeward.

The lady gazed on at elfin faced Roushni seated next to her, as the young girl concentrated happily at the traffic, engrossed animatedly humming an enchanting tune under her breath.

'She was born to sing!' The senior lady reminisced dreamily.

'Hope I have done a good job?' The mom thought still gazing admiringly at the wonder sitting next to her. That very moment Roushni happened to look at her. Their eyes locked and both smiled at each other.

Her mom took note of every ounce of her grown up child, including the transparent yellow colored add-on in her ear lobe which was a permanent part of her body now! Roushni sang from the muscle memory and vibrations with the help of hearing plugs for clarity of sound and words.

In the midst of traffic, the vehicle moved slowly, and the senior lady closed her eyes as the memories flooded back. She fell into a deep journey of reminiscence. Rewind 19 years--------

It was the 8.45 train from Bandra station. She had to reach for a presentation at 9.45. She wanted to rake into an earlier one but could not. Her baby was colicky and was not leaving her.

She was Sakshi, a 30-year old middle-class working woman from Mumbai. What she earned made a lot of sense to her home and her plate. She was responsible for that extra morsel that had to be brought to the table. Her salary supported the three of them. Her husband, herself and the tiny bundle of joy that they could not afford to have for a long time.

Her life was anything but ideal. Her days were similar except for a doctor's visit for the baby's vaccination. She squeezed these visits into her busy schedule. Before having her little Roushni, she would do a couple of hours of overtime. But now it was impossible. She could work late during her pregnancy too as that allowed her to get into a later local that was not crowded.

It was the month of June and the rains had just started. As she made into the heavily crowded train her silk sari had already soaked hugging her body at wrong places. She was however far from worrying about it than the worry at hand, as how to get into the over-crowded local train. The presentation was heavily playing on her mind too. She was sure the slides were in place but as a P.R manager she was entirely responsible for the ongoing event for her company. She was very much responsible for an overall deal with clients. Along with the corporate events and product launch, Sakshi managed the company's website too. She was the developer of content, decided the design, put up upcoming events and wrote bombastic headlines. She created captions for the hoardings as well, that are used for promoting the company from time to time. She was all rolled into one person. Overall a very hectic task but she loved it.

Before to this, she worked as a journalist in a local paper. She took up P.R as she envisioned that keeping up with the busy madness of a journalist's life after marriage would be impossible.

As a journalist she had travelled extensively, reported and been successful. She had seen it all and done it all, so she decided that it was time she hung her boots and took up a lesser mad job that required her to be on her toes all the time.

She was not very right though! Media management, content and event management needed a lot of attention even though she had some sane days unlike reporting.

Right now, Sakshi was stuck between two fat women in the ladies' compartment; she was still near to the entrance from where she had got in. She desperately pushed her way in search of a seat. Every day, she could mostly get to sit for a good 15 min before her destination arrived which was Nariman point. Her mobile started to ring. She could feel it inside her pouch and was sure that it must be her husband as he called often at that time to check if she could get in safely.

She could push herself a bit more squeezing in-between the bosoms as women grumbled under their breath. This way she was pretty sure that by the time she would get out, her clothes would be crumpled so will be her hair. She decided to quickly powder herself before aligning. Her mind raced back to the presentation again. Sakshi scrutinized herself in the small mirror that she carried in her pouch. She dabbled in more compact and looked up as a woman in the front gave a nod and her eyebrows went up; sure-sign that she looked good. Sakshi applied a long-winged liner next and went on to do that for her right eye. She then closed her eyes, allowing it to dry. She got a seat to sit after a while as the train was half empty by then.

The day looked good. One of those days when the pleasant rains watered the plants and trees making them greener. The flowers shown in all colors from the top branches of tall trees. A few low dark clouds hung around shielding the sun from showing through. Sakshi looked ravishing in a soft purple banana silk sari with a high collared blouse to boot. The pleasant color came on to her cheeks making them look pink and her husband of five years had turned romantic in the morning too after she draped it for the day. Sari wearing was a rare commodity for her, but she missed those silks hanging in her closets whenever she would browse through contemplating the dress code.

One thing was very sure: Whenever she draped one, her husband looked at her like an adolescent in love, she loved it and that was incentive enough for her to drape one sometimes. Few seconds later she called her neighbor who was taking care of her daughter.

"Hi Nandita!"

"Yes Sakshi."

"I might be late today since there are a couple of presentations and the clients will be around after that."

"No Problem, Roushni is happy with me just let me know when you will be back as I might go out to buy a couple of things from the D'Mart by maybe 5? As you know I will be carrying Roushni along."
"No problem! I will not be home today before seven. So, don't worry. Oh yes! I thought Roushni's body felt warm to me. Forgot to give you the Crocin syrup in case she develops fever..."

"I have it at home. I will give her if I sense her temperature rising."

Nandita was a nice lady in her early thirties with toddler twins on tow. Since she was not a very ambitious career woman and enjoyed taking care of her two children, she offered to take care of little Roushni when Sakshi had to resume work after her maternity leave. That way Sakshi was peaceful that her baby was in good hands.

Nandita's toddlers had just joined their school nearby. Nandita had a full-time maid who took care of the three children. She was free to move out and go about her daily errands, including the kitty parties.

Sakshi looked out as the train was slowing to a halt. Church-gate station was arriving. She cut the call after a few pleasantries bidding her friend as she had to get out.

She took her briefcase and her bag aligned, from the local and walked towards her office with purpose. Forgetting the worries of home and walking into a new day.

She reached the building in ten minutes walking fast and checked the time. It was almost 9.15. She had just around half an hour to get the monitor going for her presentation. She was pretty sure Nandu dada, the peon would have set it up for her by the time she steps into the conference hall.

She waited restlessly for the lift.

She locked her fingers as she stood. She needed those extra minutes to decide the last-minute arrangements in the presentation room. One of her colleagues ran towards the lift too as it neared the ground floor. As the door opened both Sakshi and the elderly lady accountant walked in along with a couple of men.

"Wow sari..." exclaimed Mrs. Nair- the accountant. Sakshi smiled.

"Yes, thought of it at the last minute! Tired of the pants that I wear to the office and the black and white suits for the presentations. It's high time I needed some change."

The elderly accountant looked approvingly and gave a huge nod.

"Saris are all time great dress for any occasion."

Sakshi agreed wholeheartedly.

Their floor came.

The whole office on the seventh floor was a huge space, spanning around 4000 sq. meters. On the entrance read 'RM' PR and Promotions.
Sakshi along with Mrs. Nair walked in.

"I will walk to my cubicle now. Let's meet for lunch! Hey all the best for the presentation!" Exclaimed Mrs. Nair.

Sakshi nodded unmindful as already the

apprehension of presenting weighed strong on her mind. Mrs. Nair occupied a far-off cubicle in the huge office hall while Sakshi sat at the farthest end. They hardly interacted except for the occasions when they crossed each other. Otherwise during lunch, they did exchange a few eateries.

She walked to her cubicle and landed her huge bag with the lap top and other things on the table. Jubin from the next cubicle or Jaby as he liked to be called, peeped in.

"Hey Sakshi! How is it going?"

"Hi Jaby… li'l tensed of the presentation. Need to run to check on the monitor. Want to come?" Rejoined Sakshi.

"Why not?"

Jubin was also into promos and hoarding designing, so he sat through most presentations of Sakshi. He was a closet gay and only a few knew about it including her. Now with the changing social scenario people were cool about it in the media circles. But still, as there were speculations in the outside world and the close friends were very protective about him, lest that could be a case for humiliation.

Sakshi and Jaby crossed to the presentation hall. The hall was lit and the chairs in two rows on either side occupied the room. At the farthest end stood the screen and the monitor in the centre of the rows. Sakshi smiled at Nandu and she was sure the stage was set for the day as usual. Everything seemed perfect. A few guys from the clients' side were present too. They were in animated discussion, seated informally, at the farthest end of the hall in a corner.

That day she was to make a presentation for the launch of a dog food product in the market. It was a rare promo not very typical to their organization as they dealt generally with book launching or corporate promos and events.

Today's product was 'Bark foods'. That was the name of the company too. Sakshi scrutinized herself in the glass windows. She okayed herself! A quick run to the adjoining rest room saw her coming out with a dash of fresh purple lip color that matched her beautiful silk sari and a touch of kohl!

The clients were arriving, and they were on time. The room filled up. They expected around 30 people in all including her colleagues with senior management. The presentation was to start max by 10 o'clock and she was pretty much ready too. She inserted the pen drive and the first picture of a beautiful Labrador with other breed of dogs popped. A few people in the room looked up distracted from the small chat and immediately interest could be discerned on their faces. They went back again to their humming discussions.

Her boss and a few senior marketing personnel came in. They wished her luck and went back to stand at a corner discussing some great corporate promo that they had witnessed somewhere in New York. From where she was standing, Sakshi could only hear the words 'Event!' 'New York.'

She felt nervous. Though she had made a lot of presentations still each was different and presented with fresher challenges. She looked skywards for inspiration and strength.

The room slowly filled up.

The monitor started. The small gathering of people settled with the clients in the fore front and the others in the back seats. Her clients were a huge Multinational distributor and they wanted to promote their new product in the market globally. More visibility for her with the clients meant a huge hike and a promotion. She looked up skyward, while she prayed inward.

The lights dimmed, people looked expectantly. Her eyes spanned around. Wobbly at her knees, she mustered strength from the innate quality that nature bestowed on her as a tremendous speaker, who could capture the attention of a huge audience freezing them spellbound. She lived for those thriving moments; when they happened; her work meant all!

With a sign from Nandu and Jaby, she started.

"Ladies' and Gentlemen… I am not a dog nutrition and a label reading expert. I don't own a dog as a pet and never did. In a city like Mumbai, where parents are working and for a child to own a pet, is definitely a luxury."

All nodded in unison. Some looked curiously on at the unusual start to her speech.

"But still we all crave for that connectivity with nature and pets bring in a sense of belonging in a make believe dry modern existence. I agree that a home is definitely complete with a pet! How many of you endorse my belief?"

All agreed in unison and some hands rose.

She continued now with vigor and more confidence.

"I am an animal lover and it's seen that 39% more households, own a dog in the U.S. as compared to India. However, what with the changing scenario of increasing pet owners in the metros of our country? As a responsible pet owner, I am sure I want to give the best to my Dog."
She fidgeted at this juncture with her bangle and focused full throated, on the slides.

Burden of nervousness declining she found herself more at ease. The flow of her thoughts aligned, and she could see people in the room more attentive. She knew now she had the power to manipulate with words. She went on suddenly her natural hum taking over.

"The other day I was in a lift in my building that was occupied by one of my neighbors. This particular neighbor I do not see very often but owns a dog." She smiled looking around as the client looked at her curiosity brimming.

"Naturally as this gentleman came in with a huge Golden retriever, I backed off! More out of intimidation. The dog started to growl, and I was a picture to behold." People started to look amused.

"I must have looked funny but stood my ground collecting my wits and nervousness in a trembling state." Some soft laughter.

"I must have really looked funny but went on to comment bravely to the owner of this great huge dog." The crowd cackled and Jaby almost laughed.

Sakshi continued, "Your Dog is beautiful. I am sure it's a great breed?"

"It's a golden retriever." The proud owner said disapprovingly. "Besides it's not a dog!"

I looked at the owner and the dog and must have had an expression of "What the…Fish?"

Some people chuckled.

Sakshi was saying. "Next I knew why the owner had a disapproving expression on his face in spite of my golden words for his dog?"

The client almost said. "Why?"

"This is not a dog. It's a member of my family! Its name is Messy!" At that point the dog barked twice. As if to say, 'That is my name, did you understand?' As it happens you know in the Hindi movies when the dogs bark at the wrong doers?" By this time the gathering was into guffaws. Sakshi continued in the same breath. "I did not know how to overcome this messy situation though!"

"Oh! That was all I could manage looking like an idiot." She went on effortlessly.

"By then our destination had arrived and the disapproving owner and his growling four-legged member of the family went off the lift leaving me in a baffle."

"Imagine calling his dog a family member? Taking offense too if they call him one?"

"That day the watchman had a similar amused

expression as you people have right now looking at me!" She paused for effect as the sentences seeped in the brainwaves of the crowd and it was incredulous with amusement.

"That is the very reason we are here people." She continued ever so confidently. "If a pet owner considers his dog as a member of his/her family then I think he/ she would love to feed it with the best, even better than what he/she crams down."

After that, the presentation was a cake walk. Clients were most forthcoming with their questions and there was a big chance that Sakshi's company was going to do the promos for the product that would run in millions of dollars, world over.

After the whole two hours of grilling question and answer session Sakshi came out of the conference hall elated and satisfied. A small crowd had gathered outside. It was almost lunch time and her colleagues were gearing up for food.

Jaby came forward to congratulate her on her wonderful address.

"Hey girl it was awesome! I loved it!! Where on earth do you come up with such lovely analogues? Every time I am floored!"

Sakshi just shrugged happily. The word of a

wonderful product talk had got around. Her boss and the vice presidents of both the companies (the client and hers) happened to pass.

They stopped by.
Her boss Mr. Raman was all broad smiles.

"It was a great presentation!" He shook hands.

The vice president of her company rejoined. "Please come and see me in my cabin right now!"

Sakshi nodded nervously. Her boss was all smiles and thumbs up.

Mrs. Nair, Jaby, Nandu and all others congratulated her and Mrs. Nair added.
"Sakshi Promotion pakka!"

Sakshi just nodded collecting her bag from her cubicle while proceeding on to the Vice-president's room.

She collected her thoughts about the product and the questions that may follow.

She knocked lightly on nearing the door.

"Come in!" came a curt rejoinder.

She entered gingerly and Mr. Lobo was not alone.

A couple of clients and the Vice -president of the client's company were there too.

She was ushered in to take a seat and she did cautiously pulling a chair to herself.

The people around were all smiles. While Mr. Lobo Introduced her to the clients personally others threw admiring glances at her.

"He is Mr. Subramaniam Vice President Bark Pet Foods."

Sakshi stood up and shook hands.

She also shook hands with the other two men. The men exchanged their visiting cards. Sakshi did the same.

"I am glad you made a presentation that could strike a chord with the buyer's market."

"Thank you, sir! I am happy you liked it." Sakshi rejoined. After which the clients took leave.

Mr. Lobo accompanied them to the door. After seeing them off Mr.Lobo turned to Sakshi.

"They want to hire us for the marketing promos and all the other campaigns." He informed.

"They have been searching for a good promotion

company and now after listening to at least 70 presentations they have zeroed in on us. When they confirm officially, I will let you guys know. You made an awesome product show and the questions were tackled in one hell of a great way too." Mr. Lobo pumped Sakshi's hand with enthusiasm.

She was so elated that she could not speak.

"This deal meant a lot for the company! I am considering promoting you to the position of Vice-President sales and promos. From today on a hike of 30% to your existing salary will be added."

Sakshi was speechless!

"Thank you, Sir!" She could manage excitement bubbling in her vocal cords!

She breezed out of the room smiling from ear to ear.

The day went fast, and the evening downed, she did not bother taking a train home. She hopped into a cab. As it is always with her when she was a bundle of happy sharing spree with all and sundry, in her ecstatic moments. She did not want to waste time waiting for the local and to squeeze in and out of the overloaded carriages.

She reached with renewed energy.

"I am afraid Roushni has high fever. I gave the

Benadryl syrup." Nandita said even before Sakshi could share her achievement happiness. Next, her face fell from being wide and happy to a small morsel of contortion.

"No worries I will take her to the doc." said she while collecting her li'l drowsy bundle.

She wasted no time and called a cab to the doctor's clinic nearby.
As little Roushni slept on the examining table Sakshi looked on anxious.

The doctor, a middle-aged Mr. Chaturvedi, deftly examined Roushni's little body while the mother held her. The little baby squirmed in agitation in her sleep and almost woke up.

"I am afraid it's the seasonal flu." Finally, the doctor confirmed.

"Ok"

"I will write a couple of meds and just monitor her temperature."

"Yes"

The doctor looked at Roushni's file and nodded.

As he was examining, his hand hit against the tray

full of surgical appliances next to the examination table. It fell crashing to the floor making a loud noise. The noise was enough for a sleeping panda to wake and look.

Suddenly, the doctor's eyes fell on Roushni who had gone back to sleep peacefully. His face had an expression of quizzical enquiry that is only there on a person with a deep doubt. Sakshi on her part never noticed anything. She had retreated back a step after the initial minutes as the doc was comfortable examining the little body.

Next Sakshi knew that the doctor had stopped examining and took a sterilizing tray and started hitting it with a small appliance, as if he was playing a low-key drum! That really surprised her, and she took a step forward quizzically.

The doc continued to make noise near to the sleeping baby. Though she was tired after a hectic day she wanted to laugh. How funny was this? Why was she here and what was happening? The doctor beating a drum near to the baby's face was a funny scene.

'There were no people around or it would be a funny act.' Sakshi thought. The noise continued, the Doc had a solemn expression on his face, the mother looked on amused.

Finally, the medic broke his silence about his unlikely behavior.

"Did you notice anything odd about the baby?"

"She is a peaceful baby! Mr. Chaturvedi." Sakshi responded with pride. "She does not get perturbed very fast. She is going to be cool." Mother provided unnecessarily.

"No! I am sorry. I have not seen anything that is different in her. She is a bundle of Joy for us!" The solemn expression of the doctor continued, while the mom looked on with pride. The doc prescribed the general medicines for the fever and finally broke his silence on his own noise making endeavor.

After that, her mind raced like a galloping horse all the way home.

She reached home and put her bundle on the sofa. Sakshi was no more joyful as before! That day was really beautiful. She had a promotion coming up. She had won a deal for her employer. It was like winning a Nobel prize! Now it did not matter.

By now Roushni was wide awake! Her baby lay there smiling up at her. Sakshi looked down at the smiling innocent angel. Her little one crooned happily.

The long croonings were so often with her eight-month-old that the couple had decided to make little Roushni a singer.

Sakshi's eyes moistened.

She ran into the kitchen with a tear dropping and came back armed with a steel plate and a spoon which she started to bang loudly. She was at it for only a couple of minutes when the door-bell rang. She went to open it without thinking much. There he was standing, her dear spouse smiling down.

Looking at her with a spoon and a huge steel plate he started to laugh. Looking up sheepishly with a wet cheek was Sakshi with a 'so do you know what happened?' expression.

"What the…!" He stopped short.

"Nothing."

She retraced her steps fast in with the plate and spoon banging.
"I return home one day to find my woman going mad banging a plate?" He moved his head laughing.

"Please don't tell me that this is one of your many ideas of a mating ritual that you watched on TLC? Are we going to have a great night today?" Her husband said as he pulled her to him next with the bag and files sliding down to the floor.

He looked at the smiling blissful face of his baby on the sofa to his wife. After disentangling, Sakshi started to bang while the blissful baby crooned.

"Oh! I understand you are giving music to the crooning that she is into! Ha ha." He added laughing!

As the father came into the baby's focus, the smile and the croon widened.
Sakshi started to bang on the utensil a little louder as her husband picked the baby from the couch as if to save it from a mad woman.

"What are you doing?" He asked finally agitated.

"Can you not see what you missed all these months?"

"What?" Her husband said defensively.

She brought the sound nearer. The baby's expression did not change at the banging sound, but she smiled at Sakshi and looked on from one parent to the other with a slightly baffled look.

"Did you notice something?"

Sakshi went on with the sound as before.

"Have you gone mad?"

"We had not but we discovered something today. Our Doc did!"

Her husband smoothed the hair off the little forehead.

"What? You are banging this utensil too near to the baby."

"That is what exactly I am trying to show you!"

"What, What?!"

By now Roushni who was suffering from a slight temperature was uncomfortable. She had a quizzical expression and an irritated disposal and started to whimper.

"She is crying! stop this…!" He almost ran to the other room with the little girl and Sakshi followed with the banging unfazed. Wherever he went she followed. It became a funny game till he stopped near to their bed.

"My ears are bursting."

"But hers are not!"

"Sakshi something has come over you?"

"Nothing!" By now Sakshi had put the things that she was carrying on the side table and started to weep softly.

"Oh! What? What happened? Darling what happened? Tell me what happened?" Her spouse realized that something had taken place in his absence. Otherwise everyday was a hunky dory one with Sakshi well into her culinary putouts by the time he arrived famished.

"Can you see? My little angel is…is…!"

"Of course! I can, the little angel and also your mad angle. What is it?
What is going on?"

"Cannot you see it?"

"What?"

"Please Harshad, just see how our baby is reacting?"

"Yes?"

"After all the noise?"

The baby had an irritable disposal by now and started to whimper and cry.

"In this kind of a sound you get irritable, I get irritated? But then how a small ear drum cannot?" She said.

"Oh God!" cried out Harshad.

"Did you see it?"
"Oh God! I, I?"
"Oh God!"

"Oh my God!"

While the baby whimpered the young parents held on to each other crying.

"You mean, you mean our baby cannot? You mean…"

"Possibility that she cannot! We need to take her to an ENT specialist!"

"Cannot believe this is happening to us! She has lately started to speak some words…"

"We need to take her to a doc."

Forward 18 Years---

Roushni walks out of the London school of Music for deaf.

She is the topper of her college. When so many years back the ENT child specialist in Lilavati had pronounced Roushni as partially deaf and it would take anytime from 10 to 20 years or less to totally lose hearing.

Sakshi's life was overturned. In that painful topsy

turvy situation she had looked deep into the cherubic face and determined to make the little soul someone that the world will know one day!

"Atleast! I will try." Her husband had pressed her hand till his knuckles pained. It was support enough.

She had tried her level best in the early years to inculcate as many sounds and words and languages she could teach little Roushni, she did. When she got a seat in the Royal college of London for singing and music, Roushni was almost deaf at eighteen. She had learnt at least six languages, Marathi- her mother tongue, English, Hindi, French, Spanish and Tamil. Just into her first year, Sakshi had noticed her little one crooning along whenever she heard or watched music. Sure enough, Roushni loved music and songs as she grew. She had this extraordinary gift of a talent her parents realized when she won an inter-school singing competition in early years. There were no doubts in the mind of these young parents.

Sakshi left no stone unturned to make Roushni a full-fledged singer.

Present day-------

"Cannot believe!" They whispered in the dark, as they saw Roushni in the recording studios. "Cannot believe Harshad that she is such a beautiful singer. Her first song sold one million copies Harshad!" She whispered almost to herself.

Harshad had nothing to say but nodded through the wetness of his own   lashes. He was happy he was sitting there witnessing the vision manifest in front of them.

The two shadows had just squeezed each other's hands as the music flowed into them.

Sakshi looked at Roushni from the corner of her eye now! She smiled happily to herself!

She had dreamt big for her baby but this big? Dreams do come true! The vehicle turned at a corner and they entered the gates to their building.

❊ ❊ ❊

STORY - 2

Acceptance

Sam was unhappy with the way he had designed the hoardings. He was working on them for most of the day with much innovation with less results to his satisfaction. Most of his colleagues somehow felt otherwise though.

He scrutinized the designs for the last time with no further creativity taking over. It was a Friday and he had to meet a friend in one of the Mumbai bars for a drink. His back was breaking, and head seemed empty! Sam could not bring the adrenaline rush anymore! Simply exhausted he decided to wind up for the day!

He was in his late 20s and unmarried. He loved spending time with friends in the evenings specially on Fridays. Today was that day! He shut the machine and looked up at the watch. It was 7 after dusk. He had just about half an hour to reach the pub that he wanted to visit.

He got up and took his coat and zipped his work bag. Turning his phone to a silent mode, walked to the rest rooms. Once there apart from the work worn eyes, he approved himself. The gold streaks in his long shoulder length hair were expertly hidden for the office hours. He brushed his fingers through to give volume to the mane, to bring out the streaks. Satisfied after a few strokes, he scrutinized again. The brown eyes and chiseled features reflected back a handsome 'Greek God' look that could easily turn a saint on. He took one last scrutiny and moved out!

Sam was a client services representative and led a team. He was a talented, avid speaker and a great PR professional. He was a six-footer, dark brown eyed fellow, who owned it all and worked his way up in the advertising world. He loved his job. His colleagues often reprimanded and ragged him about his handsome single status. He shrugged it away with a smile most often.

Presently, he walked out with deft strides, looking regal and handsome. He got into a waiting cab. The taxi maneuvered itself slowly out of the traffic. His office at Nariman point was a busy suburb in down town area and he had to reach the pub at Marine Lines, perched high up on the 22nd floor of a sky scraper. The cab moved at a snail's pace. The vehicles almost brushed against one another! Sam became restless sitting inside!

The evening had set in and the sky was crimson at the horizon. After reaching Marine lines the cab sped in less traffic. The vendors had all put out the wares and the evening walkers were everywhere on the promenade by the sea. Children, young moms, old women and men, practicing marathon runners, all seemed to throng the place with activity and vitality.

The taxi moved for quite some time. He looked into his watch. It was 15 min since he had taken the cab. He looked over the front seat craning his neck to have a better view of the location. He was almost there. The google map showed. He directed the driver to pull up at a 25-story building after entering a by lane. The driver did.

Sam paid the cab and walked deftly towards the entrance. The place was the trendiest with skyscrapers, in town area and as very characteristic of Mumbai city, was hidden in the small lanes. The building was an exclusive 25 floors with supersonic glass capsule lifts. It towered over others in the vicinity and a view to behold. He waited with a couple of foreign guests and some visitors on entering. The lift took him up in a minute. Sam switched off his phone that had many missed calls and WhatsApp messages. He decided to glean them later and resigned himself for the evening!

He walked out with a bouquet of beautiful red roses bound in pink paper, he had picked at the junction. He scanned the restaurant with eagle eyes. A broad smile broke over his face as he located Jess seated on a high chair at a corner, facing the sea by the French windows. He stood out even if he was seated, regal and beautiful. On reaching Jess, he pecked him on the cheek.

Sam gave him roses.
Jess made a face.

"Did you speak to your parents about moving out?"

"No, not yet!" Sam replied.

"I don't know when you are going to do it?"

"Very shortly! Please don't be angry with me!"

"I am working on all this. My moving out, us and living separate."

He sat next to Jess pulling the high wine counter stool. Jess was his lover of two years and both were deeply involved. They regularly argued with the topic of living in together.

Sam's parents did not know a thing. They did not know of his sexual preferences either.

Both settled next to one another holding hands.

Sam looked deep into Jess's eyes. He could see a tear drop to the cheek of his lover. It was rainy season and the sea outside, rose up and down as the high tide broke against the rocks tirelessly. Both the lovers, hand-in-hand gazed at the ocean for some time. Jess with a blank expression while Sam wondering at the beauty of nature. Jess thought desperately,

'Nature was so accepting.'

The odd couple sat quietly.

The lifeless rocks silently bore with the oceans rage. The muddy waves transformed into white foam as they hit against them. The whole nature looked wonderfully beautiful and surrendered.

"Surrender we must." said Sam to Jess. "What else can we do? Even today in India, gay couples are not accepted in the society."

"Though we live in an existing time of renewal and change, it will take long for the Indian society to accept us." Sam found himself say.

Jess looked at him with sadness all written on his face.

"You know my problem is not it?" Jess rebound.

"Yes?"

"I cannot live without you and the pressure of my parents for me to get married is very high. Almost driving me mad!" Countered Jess.

Sam could understand as his parents were equally devastated when he announced that he had chosen not to marry for life. They could not understand why but that was what he had told them. It took them several months to accept and not show him so called 'Good Matches' for marriage.

They had no clue whatsoever that he was gay. That was another, hurdle he needed to cross next. But time seemed to really pass by and sand seemed to slip away as much they wanted to hold it.

Both sat for some time hand-in-hand. As their drinks arrived, they sipped quietly. That was the beauty of their relationship. They did not speak much but understood a lot.

Time ticked slowly by. Still it was two hours that they sat together speaking less, feeling intensely and touching each other intermittently. They needed to get back home. Jess lived nearby. He was a towny all his life while Sam was a Bandra boy.

"I need to see my doc tomorrow." Jess was saying.
"Why?"

"I am having a lot of problem breathing."
"Oh! I feel you should stop smoking. I always had a problem with that."

"I know. I will."

"When?"

Jess did not reply. Both sipped at the Vodka on rocks.

Two Years Later..

The sea flashed against the rocks outside. The weather was terribly bad. In the hot May month, the summer storm was brewing up. The weather seemed to be angry. So much so that, the sound of waves could be heard into the small cubicle in the hospital room.

Sam looked at the immobile body. He was unresponsive to the world, the weather and the storm. A storm raged inside of him too. Tears welled time-to-time. His partner Jess was fighting the last stages of cancer in his lungs. He was fresh out of another surgery and was on sedatives. Doctors could not say much about what would happen to him at that time. This was already the third surgery in 6 months and the deadly disease had spread to the other parts of his body. Jess's limp body on the bed looked dead. Sam for some reason knew what would be. He just knew!

Jess was immobile for a long time. After the last operation the previous evening he was mostly immobile. Jess's strained breathing filled the room! The occasionally moving ventilator a proof of his existence, added on to Sam's anxiety.

Presently the doc came for his regular visit. He gingerly stepped in and checked the instruments around Jess's body. He nodded at Sam.

"Pray for his recovery." He nodded again, "Nothing can be said right now!"

Sam nodded. Jess's parents looked after him very well, but they were old and depended on the hospital and friends for further support. In their view Sam was a great help.

They obviously did not know the truth.

On the other hand, Sam's parents knew that he was gay by now, but they were far from understanding their child's sexual orientation. His mother was devastated for giving birth to an abnormally dysfunctional boy and the father did not know what to say for a long time except that he would repeat again and again.

"What the society would think and say about this!" So far to dissuade any speculation, Sam decided to remain a closet gay.

Sam's parents mourned the death of their normal child who was never going to get married and bring in the grandchildren! After months of grieving, they finally accepted him, and they were doing above average in the grief barometer according to him.

Sam looked at the still body of his lover inside the ventilator with longing. He wanted to cry aloud but could not. He wanted to tell the world what he was going through, about his fears and premonitions.

The only thing he did was to remain still and observe the chest heave up and down inside the machine that looked like a trapped bird.

After the doc left, Sam put his head to the side of the bed and fell into a deep slumber. It must be mid-afternoon when he was woken by a sound. He realized that Jess's breathing was the reason. He was breathing more than the regular strained tempo that he was, post operation. In a moment of sudden development, Jess opened his eyes and the sound stopped. It was the stillness that Sam felt was so different from the otherwise quietude of the room. He understood. He stared at the limp body and he shuddered uncontrollably so as the wetness on his cheeks increased. He did not bother to raise an alarm. He just sat there whispering sweet nothings to his sweetheart!

Fast forward---2 years to the present day!

A solo performance by a handsome guitarist ended. Sam observed from his corner every note and move of the artist. His hands went up to give an ovation as the performance concluded. It was the high-end night club in town, jam packed with guests of all nationalities. The table he seated on was occupied. His parents had accompanied him that day!

Denis was the performer for the day. He was a French guitarist of reasonably popular fame. The crowd was applauding in the end of the rendition and he bowed in acknowledgement.

After the guitarist walked, a vocalist came on to the stage. She was a British singer of Hispanic origin. She started crooning as a preamble as Denis moved away from the centre. The crowd was getting warmed up to her performance and the guitarist receded through the exit.

As the night moved on, Sam and his parents enjoyed the music and the food. They were greeted by a guest after a while.

"We loved your music today like always." Sam's mom hugged as Denis joined them at the table after his performance.

"Thanks Ruby!"

Sam's papa smiled and shook hands with him.

"Lovely!" He gushed while Denis nodded smiling.

Intermittently, guests looked in their direction and some recognized Denis and smiled and waved. He waved back!

Denis, Sam, Sam's mom and Dad shared the food, joked and listened to the music and generally enjoyed the over-crowded, smoke-filled night club and togetherness.

Sam's parents were old fashioned Catholics of Goan origin and they did not agree to Sam's sexual preferences, so he had to remain a closet gay! Now they had come around. What with Sam's dream of adopting kids or having test tube babies, their desire of becoming grandparents was not far away!

'Indian society is looking at these issues and choices more openly now!' His parents felt! They had stopped bugging Sam and moved on, in acceptance! Life had come a full circle for every one of them!!

As for Sam he enjoyed being with his new soul mate Denis and they spent as much of time as they could together in their love pad! Denis travelled the world as a guitarist and they roamed places in their free time together.

"This is change and it is always difficult!" Sam's papa would often acknowledge to his mom. Then they would nod in unison.
On the other hand, Sam enjoyed the strings of a guitar and a new life!

✳ ✳ ✳

STORY - 3

Courage

"I told you to keep the glass in the overhead shelf not here?" Boomed Raghav.

Soumya obliged obediently.

Raghav and Soumya were married for 5 years. Their relationship was the relation of dreams. She was out of an abusive relationship and had met with Raghav in a social club. They hit it off immediately! He was a friend of a friend and seemed to be everything a woman ever dreamt of! Six months of meetings and partying led to their first date. It was in a five-star hotel. Though the food was not so great the candles added to the mystery and led to their first kiss. It felt magical to Saumya!

"This and more I really want with you!" Said Raghav after they kissed several times after the first. Saumya had blushed a beetroot red. Their courtship continued for another six months, before Raghav proposed to her. She was very explicit and told him all about her abusive previous relationship with her classmate and he was more than sympathetic.

"You are such a gem of a person. I don't understand why someone would be abusive to you?" He had remarked surprised!

Saumya knew that very moment that she had found her man. She made it sure that he knew everything about her life before jumping in. He was more than understanding to what she told about her failed relationship. They were made for each other. After a while both the parents gave their green signals and the marriage took place. Their life was a bed-of-roses after that. In the first year itself, Saumya miscarried their first baby. It was a fluke pregnancy, so they let it pass.

"I feel vacant inside sometimes!" Saumya would muse to Raghav.
"It is natural to feel that way. Since we were not prepared for parenthood maybe someone up there heard it. It's ok!" He would reassure her with a hand over hers.

As days passed, the work pressures caught on and they became like two working maniacs under the same roof. As workaholics both, loved their work to no end!

Saumya was a dog groomer. She went back to it. The salon was open from 10 in the morning to 8 in the evening. That kept her on her toes. Her line of duties included suggesting the right kind of shampoo, soap and grooming ingredients for pooches of all sizes and breeds.

Grooming also included the right way of shampoo, trimming of nails to teeth, ear cleaning of the four-legged pets. Most of the animals were dogs sometimes cats walked in too. They were shampooed, cleaned, trimmed off their excessive mane and nails.

Saumya looked after the complete beautification and grooming and suggested remedies for daily maintenance challenges faced by the owners, while the staff carried out instructions. Amidst so much hectic and interesting activities she forgot about her own pain of miscarriage. Raghav became more and more restless as the days went by. He was traveling more, working long, getting less attention from his spouse that made him bitter about the things in general.

A part of him that was otherwise new to Saumya surfaced. His irritable countenances increased day by day and he would ask explanations from her for petty things around the house that he had never before.

"Why did you keep this plate here? Are you not paying attention to the house?"

"No as if you don't know I was very busy with the saloon?" Saumya would retort little perturbed herself.

"But you know that I like things in their place?"

"I know… give me a break. I am not responsible for everything. I am working as well!"

He would make a face at that, that she had never witnessed before.

"I Know… work?"

"Raghav?"

"Be home by sharp nine. I like my food fresh and hot! I am sure you know that?"

That was one of the first shocking moods of Raghav that Saumya witnessed, giving a dark phantom memory. He demanded everything that Saumya did during the day, after that he wanted to know everything about her movements; where she was, what she was doing at a particular time, whether she had reached home from work? He became more restless if she did not on time. Her cut off time was 9 and she needed to be around when he returned. He was policing everything around her.

"Don't you feel you are reaching home too late?"

"Why? That is the time of the saloon. The closing is 8."
"I know that, but it would be better if you could take up a part time job instead of this."

"Why part time? I love my job and besides you come so late! Some days you are not there."

"I want you to be early to cook and clean. The house is in a mess!"
"It's not true. Most of the work is over in the

morning. Besides is this not your home too? You can also do some work!"

On that he again made a strange face. He even stood just inches close to her with that strange look that made hair stand on her neck, that brought goose bumps of phantoms gone by! She could only relax after he had left home for work that day.

The restlessness grew slowly to taunting and snide remarks. Saumya bore the small changes and put up with the remarks.

Today particularly he was in an irritable mood and wanted everything to be in a perfect order.

"I told you to keep the glass in the overhead compartment?" He screamed. She obliged as usual. The next sentence was totally unasked for.

"What your previous boyfriend would have done?" He said totally out of context. "I am a good man so am going on putting up with this shit!"

Saumya wanted to scream back. She was dog tired after a heavy day and wanted to keep peace in the house. She had dinner to cook too. This kind of an outburst was totally unexpected. From where her previous boyfriend had cropped in? It was from such a long back? But those remarks started the alarm triggers.

This hurt her the most. Next, she knew her husband was towering over her.
"I have told you umpteenth number of times not to keep things out of place? Don't you really understand lady?"

He slapped her in a fit. She reeled under the impact and fell to the ground. In the process smashing her head against the wall in the kitchen. She stayed there for some time absorbing the shock and the turn of the event totally paralyzing her. The menacing man looked all red eyed demon like. He never looked so violent. Eyes all open, face contorted. 'He was a different entity'. She thought.

For some time, she remained where she was lying on the ground, tasting liquid salt. She felt a contraction inside her stomach so intense she wanted to puke.

She ran towards the bathroom. She emptied her guts in the toilet seat. She just sat there as the red colored liquid gave a saltish tinge to her mouth taste. She emptied more into the seat. Depleted she sat on where she was! She had no time to switch the lights on, so she sat in the darkness feeling faint! She could sense him behind her next!

"What on earth has come over you woman? What are you up to?"
'She was there puking her guts out in the pot and he was asking her what was she up to? How heartless that can sound?' She thought.

"You have lost it!" Was his next reaction. "Cannot you switch the lights on?" He switched the light and growled down all red eyed angry. The words just jabbed through her heart and into her emptied guts.

She was still in a stupor, tried to think sane!

This shift of a behavior in her spouse was totally unexpected. Next, he reached out and made her stand. That was also unexpected. Otherwise, a kind gesture, lacked its usual softness!

"What are you doing woman. Are you pretending to have fallen sick?"

This was totally unexpected too. In most times till today he was so considerate and loving. This was unfathomable. He stood there shaking her, shouting and demanding an explanation.

"You dumb girl! I told you so many times to do things right. You dumb woman?"

She covered under the mad wrath and looked at him with unassuming trepidation. He looked more ferocious more demonic. He shook her like a rag doll. This was a new face! The ugly face of a loving man! He was the exact replica of a phantom she had escaped from Or was he replicating her worst fears?

She clenched her stomach.

"What now, you are sick? Do you want to go out for dinner? You cannot cook?"

Saumya looked into the red eyes with disbelief. Last time she had fallen sick with Malaria he had taken the puke in his hands without shifting her from the bed. Today when she was sick because he hit her, he was demanding explanations?

"What woman? What happened?" He was still demanding as she stood there not because she had the strength but because he was holding her by the shoulders. Like a puppet, she swung from side to side. He pulled her out of the darkness. With whatever strength she had she escaped his clutches, dragged herself with snot still oozing out of her lips and somehow fell on the bed.

She lied there motionless, fear gripping her insides for the first time, as he growled over her cursing and abusing her from time to time.

She was one of those women who felt that the virtue of compassion was more powerful than violence. She was the one who always believed in making up and did too.

"I am not going to cook today!" She found herself say boldly. "I am not! I am very sick today and you can see it! You know that I work, and I need to be there when the clients come."

A peek into his unstable moods had just braced its ugly head for the first time. The clench fisting relaxed, but he went on in brash tones more to feed his ego than for anything else.

"I told you to keep things in order around the house." He said sitting down next to her in the gentlest way possible. She did not move. She started to count backwards. Something she mostly did to beat nervousness.

"I want the best for both of us. You know that? Don't you?" He said softly, as if nothing had happened. Saumya flinched.

She was very sure that he won't physically abuse her now. But she also knew in her heart of hearts that their relationship had shifted.

"Are you going to cook or going to order from out?" he nudged her. The wild streak seemed to brim a bit as his voice rose.

She was not understanding, she realized she did not want to fight and had no stamina to argue. He was at the worst behavior like a bipolar demon. She decided in a fit that she needed to do what she needed to.

"I will cook!" she found herself say. It was unnecessary. But she was after all an Indian woman who believed in the virtue of sacrifice more than anything else. Like most Indian women of her race beckoned her to give her best till the man's heart melts.

After lying down for some time, she washed herself to cook a meal for both of them that saw no sympathy or help from her otherwise sweet husband. The whole time, she had a painful feeling of being a shaft being drilled into her. Why did she decide to cook after she had vehemently did not want to and had announced it too? Was it that she felt going back to her words would prove fatal for their relationship? Her mind raced. As it would when the world turns around, when the heavens fall!

The next morning her coffee ritual and the breakfast went quietly. Her demon had changed before leaving for work.

"I am sorry. I love you. I am very sorry! I do not mean any of it!"
She just remained there glued without a word to say. She dragged through the days after that. Her husband was not at all physically abusive, but he would blow the lid every now and then! He would often pick on her work and the chores that she did at home! Everything became a problem.

"Are you so idiotic that you cannot do a thing right?" he would say at the slightest irritation or
"Why is this coffee so yuck?" or "Where were you when I called you at 12? I know you will say you

were busy?"

When she would retreat into her shell and would decide to leave or cry, he would say-
"You know honey that I love you? I am very sorry. I am very pissed with my boss in the office. Hope you understand?"

On other days again the same behavior continued.

He would often call her.

"You dumbo how many times to tell you? You will never improve? You brainless idiot? Why did I ever marry you? The food that you make sucks. The roadside canteen serves better idlis. You are a useless woman."

The very next day he was again all right.

Saumya was clueless as to how to make this relation work? This bi-polar of a relation was slowly drilling through her soul. She was not physically battered but his painful words punctured her sanity.

He did not like to acknowledge that she was good at anything. Not in the house nor outside.

She had started to feel bad about herself constantly! He would often snap at her and belittle in front of her friends and his friends in a party too.

The years passed. They were married for 5 long years this way. The abuse increased after the first year. It was never physical not even a finger he touched on her body after the first time he had raised his hand. It was always verbal. The intense mental torture led to a couple of abortions. Her parents were getting older day by day and more restless by the years. The marriage was not going anywhere either. The love that she experienced and felt for the man who supported her through one bad relationship to stand by her had turned her tormentor. The pain that she endured was unimaginable and the shaft that was going into her heart was deeper by each passing day! He was her dream man but now turned into a demon!

The life that she was leading was eating her slowly. She lost weight! The dark circles around her eyes were frighteningly dark! Her soul cried for sympathy! Most importantly she wanted it out.

Every time she decided it was enough, he would bring her back again. He would promise to improve, promising to be the lover once that he was! He would implore her to forgive and to forgo his bad ways. Begged apology and went back to his ways again in a few days!

She could not take a final call on their marriage. It was also because she felt weak as if someone was holding on to her feet every time she wanted to walk away! She was worked up because of the social pressures her parents put on her.

"You need to put up child a bit! Men don't have patience after a while!" Her mom often told her whenever she complained a little. Her pouring out was only a fraction of what he put her through every day!

"Really?" she thought. Her mom did not lead her life. Besides the old-fashioned counseling she was subjected to, was not in sync with any of the things that she was undergoing.

Burdening her parents was the last thing she wanted in their old age!

One day she met her best friend after office. It was a thursday and her husband Raghav was out of town. He was not expected for a couple of days more. It was the best time to meet up an old friend, someone she really looked up to. Rathika was one such woman who listened to her patiently without judgement. That time and again soothed Saumya's aching nerves. Though she met up people after work hours for a drink or so, she kept an eye out for her husband's stalking calls.

After five long years of marriage, she sneaked in small pleasures, in his absence. Her happiness was a glass of wine with a friend over a conversation! Her romance filled days were past gone and she felt like her own shadow!

"After suffering for long it becomes a habit." Her friend said over a mock tail of Vodka and Sprite. It happened to be their meeting joint after work sometimes.

Rathika was a healer by profession. Life coaching and healing was a part of Rathika's agenda.

"Life patterns are formed with continuous suffering. They continue lifetime after lifetime. If the pattern is not broken, then you are telling the abuser that it's ok you can continue to abuse me! After prolonged suffering the victim starts to identify with the tormentor!"

Saumya looked up from the drink baffled.

"What? Really? No wonder I started to feel that it is ok to be spoken to rudely sometimes!"

"That is the reason why you feel so confused and uncertain. He has not touched you or hit you ever, but the truth is he has emotionally and mentally battered you. See he has made you weak by not even laying a finger on your body harshly!"
"So true!"

"You have become emotionally incapable to break

away from the shackles of his torture. He has constantly told you how incapable you are, how useless you can be. That is abuse my dear girl."

"I am financially independent. How can I be mentally and emotionally dependent on him?" Saumya asked painfully though doubtful, knowing that there could be truth in her friends advise.

"That is the trick dear. That is how these tormentors work in breaking a person. First, they earn respect and trust but as the trust develops, they start to show their true colors. In the language of healing we call it the victim mentality. You become a victim and weak."

"God! I did not think of it. I did not know it!"

"It's not yet very late. You can still get out. It's been 5 years. If you remain for 5 more, then you will be in a bigger trouble. Ten years is a long time. Already you are late. Please try and understand that this does not make much sense!"

"I agree." Saumya nodded. But she was too weak to fight him. He had drained her off her life force- that was her confidence! She knew that she had to do it somehow! But how?
"Baby! There are heavy dark circles around your eyes. Why so? You have not been sleeping or staying awake for Raghav as he worked the nights late?"

Her mom often asked with anxiety framing her delicate face.

"Yes ma." Saumya had agreed meekly as she had no other explanation to give about her troubled marriage.

She dare not give the details of her mental torture or her father would die of heart attack. They were simple people. A divorce was unthinkable for her parents.

Saumya nodded briefly. "I need to take care to detach from this relationship. It won't be easy to leave him peacefully."

"Of course! It won't be easy! You need to plan and what I suggest is first mentally prepare on leaving him. Most people come under the emotional anxiety of leaving a partner."

"Thinking about the society and other problems thereafter. Winning over your parents or having a support system is very important. Happy that you do not have kids so far."

Thinking about walking out gave Saumya jitters really. She thought of it often after her second abortion. Her doctor had mentioned that she needed to take it easy and remain relaxed to remain pregnant. What the outside world did not know was both times she was pregnant she miscarried as the emotional turmoil escalated.

Her phone started to ring now. It was 8.30 and who else but, it was Raghav.

She started to shiver inwardly.

Rathika sensed pain as her friend's expression changed ! One moment she was all happy and another she had an expression of intense anxiety. Saumya's internal anxiety made her hands shiver.

After the first, calls came one after the other. She was in two minds. Whether to take them or not? Finally, she decided against it. Peace reigned for some time. Rathika's eagle eyes were reading her friends body language.

"What happened? Was it his call?" Saumya nodded.

"Why did not you take it?"

"It's a headache... taking his call."

"Hmm. You should take it and tell the truth. Be firm! Not defensive but firm."

Saumya nodded again. "I know but if something he says I don't like right now I would be spoiling my evening. Anyways day after he will come home to spoil my peace!"

"How long will you bear with this? You will need to take a call someday."

"I know. After meeting you I feel some sense come over me." She reached out for her friend's hand.

"I am feeling clear in my head!"
"Yep you should take a decision!"

Saumya nodded again.

"All these years I was blinded by the love for him. He cheated and played on my trust totally. He molested my individuality, made me empty inside. I am today a broken soul! I am demoralized and feel lack of confidence." Saumya vented.

"I think you need to break away as fast as possible otherwise you could be in a very big trouble. Part by part he will dismantle you. Within a few years you will be an empty shell. You will fail to recognize yourself," her friend was saying. "Nobody remains happy in it."

Saumya's grip fastened on Rathika's hand.

"You will need antidepressants and a counselor. Mental health is more important than anything in life."

Saumya nodded. But in the pit of her stomach the

pain was churning. The phone rang again! Anxiety returned.

"It's so strange once upon a time I was so eager to just take his call and today I hate to even hear from him!"

"That is karma!" her friend retorted with a rue smile."Strange! Strange it is!" she repeated.

Saumya jumped as her phone started again. Should she or should she not. The place was by now hiving with activity. There was loud music in the background, so she walked out, as she did, the phone stopped ringing.
She called back.

"Where were you?" His voice boomed.

 "I am in the car driving back." She lied. Thankfully the traffic in the background made noise.

"Hmm you are late!"
"I will call you the signal is green."

She cut the call.

After that she was not herself. She returned back to the pub, but frustration was all over her.

"What happened? What does he say?" Rathika

enquired though she knew that her friend had suffered a set-back just by speaking to her so called husband for a few minutes.

"As usual, he wanted to know if I reached home or not?"
"Hmm!"
"He was like it is already very late."
"It's late?" Rathika smirked. "Has he lost it?"
"Ya he has."

"I think it is time you have to take a stand!" Rathika insisted but did not pursue the topic further as her friend already looked disturbed.

After that the talk was general. They spoke about their lives and work.
Her husband called several times. She ran out to take a call to inform him that she was only a short distance from home, though in actuality she was still in the pub. The street traffic sound saved her.

Since she had not taken his previous calls, he had called her mom to check.

"I spoke to your mom!" Was what he said when she complained that she was home but wanted to retire for the day while in actuality she was just entering the parking lot!

"About?"

"About your whereabouts!"
"Whereabouts?" That word was like a shaft down her grey cells.

"You know very well that I was stuck in traffic?" She said it with emphasis that she was not used to in a long time. "Hmm?" was his infuriating reply.

"Your mom had no clue where you were!"

"You know Raghav that I do not report to my parents anymore?" She thought 'I am not in the 9th grade!' She yawned loudly to prove her tiredness.

It was past midnight when she finally entered home. She called her mom.
"Raghav called you?" She asked directly.

"Ya beta where were you?"

"Ma! I returned from work little late as there was traffic and fell asleep!"
Her mom bought her story.

The house was quiet except for a small noise of the water tank full of exotic fish in the living room. The fish tank emanated a dull light that reflected mostly in the living room and the passage! She switched other lights on moving in. Her small apartment emanated cozy feelings of care and comfort with a few decorative dull lights.

After a while, brushed, showered and into her night clothes she climbed into bed and pulled the bed covers close to her. Her dog, a small breed Brussels Griffon that was running around excitedly from the time of her entry, jumped on to the bed wagging its tail rapidly.

Generally, her beautiful Griffon called 'April' would sleep in the house on her mat very obediently while both were out. The keys were with the neighbors and the lady would peek in once a while and supervise. Her maid came in too and Saumya had trained her to give food and bath when she could not. It was a small breed and was trained to remain indoors. Saumya saw to it that as far as possible the pet was free, ate well and played around.

April loved kids and Saumya's neighborhood was full of children who loved the little fellow. Luckily for her, her otherwise monster husband loved pets. He took good care of April and the dog did not exhibit any signs of anxiety.
That night she just lied on the bed, staring long at the ceiling. Her A.C was on and it made a whirring sound that strangely comforted her. She looked out of the window and the moon smiled back. Though it was not a full moon's night, her glass windows reflected the beaming light from the soothing satellite.

Saumya took April on her chest and the dog

slept there in the legs-up position with a peaceful expression. A smile crossed Saumya's face. She closed her eyes, but sleep eluded her. She looked at the ceiling and April intermittently as the pet changed sides. Saumya brought her into the comforter finally and April snuggled inside the warmth with its nose close to her face like a baby. She wondered if an offspring could bring about that feeling of comfort? But the thought itself felt constricting in the given circumstances.

The comforting A.C noise was like a slow lullaby that took Saumya from consciousness to wakefulness till she drifted asleep to dream of her childhood. She was happy, carefree in it! She woke up again suddenly in the middle of the night realizing that her childhood had passed. She stared at the ceiling in the dim night lamp that reflected long shadows of the furniture around. April woke up too and looked into her eyes and went back into the folds of the comforter. Saumya went back to sleep again dreaming of Raghav with red eyes screaming expletives at her. She woke up to wet cheeks and day light.

The day was Friday and like all Fridays, she was not in a hurry. It was the fag end of the week and everybody fell into a holiday mood prior to the real weekend. She felt no different!

The door-bell rang. She lazily put her feet down and

got into the sleepers next to her bed on the floor. Saumya opened the door with a groggy yawn that escaped uninterrupted. April Followed her half way into the hall lazily too.

Saumya's maid was Shakti who lived in a nearby shack in a slum. She was honest, energetic and hardworking, who did most of the kitchen and house work that included the morning coffee and breakfast.

After Saumya retreated, the servant picked milk from the door step and walked into the kitchen.

While brushing she made cerebral calculations of the day's client commitments realizing that she could take it a little easy. Unable to shrug the laze and the previous night's hang over, she finally decided to work from home. That could be possible by guiding her staff from where she was.

'I will just guide the girls from here. I as well rest and take it easy before Raghav comes back!' She decided.

The thought of Raghav again gave jitters that never failed to worry her, despite the fact that once she crazily loved him and restlessly waited for his return!

'I will call up the clients later and inform about my

absence.' She thought again.

'Besides December is a lazy month and sometimes the appointments got cancelled. Hopefully today is that day!' She sheepishly smiled at her own thoughts and walked slowly towards the bedroom.

She could hear sounds from the kitchen as she got into bed once more feeling lousy. She pulled the covers over herself. April jumped on to her again, nuzzling close. Saumya just lied on the bed for the heck of it. As the morning activity in the kitchen progressed, she waited for her coffee. After half an hour she was woken up by her maid with a huge cup in hand. She had slept fitfully for some time.

"Madam, please drink this?" Shakti was almost loud in the quiet room.

"Oh!" Saumya opened her eyes in a flash and looked around. She took the cup from the maid gingerly.

"I am making Poha for today's breakfast!"

"Yes .Ok. Ah!"

Shakti went back to making breakfast while Saumya got out of the comforter and walked slowly into the seating area sipping the hot brew.

"Please make food for April?" Saumya instructed

Shakti.

"Yes Madam. I am making it. Porridge is almost ready."

The oats were imported specially from Germany. It was April's favorite breakfast.

Shakti finished making the porridge and Poha at the same time and served them both and made her own tea. April ate away at the porridge in slurps of eager licks, making sounds out of the dish it was served in her corner of the hall, as Saumya almost gulped spoonfuls of yummy poha.

"Please come here and drink your tea." Offered Saumya to the maid.
Generally, the maid sat on her own as she and Raghav had their breakfast on the table.

"Come here Shakti?" Saumya called out again. The maid came into the seating area and sat down with her cup.

"Sit on the carpet. It is very cold!"

Shakti came on to the carpet with her cup.

"How is your family?" Saumya enquired.

"Good Madam!"

Shakti had a physically abusive spouse. That she often cried about to her employer.

"How is your husband?" Saumya smiled. She could not speak much about herself as her own Raghav had turned out to be someone she did not know.

"Is he good with you? Your husband? Does he still drink and hit you?"

Shakti was shaking her head.

"What?"
"He drinks madam but does not hit me anymore? He is a changed man!"

"Oh! Very good. She rejoined to double, "What?! Does he still scream at you then? Abuse?"

"No madam!"

"How long he is been good now?"
"Chhe mahine." (Six Months)

Saumya's eyebrows came together quizzically. Embroiled in her own problems, she had not taken a look at her maid of late.
'She looks peaceful to me.' She observed.

"What! Did you do something or it just? What?"

"You have office madam?"

"No today I have taken a leave. Please tell me I have a lot of time."

Shakti looked hesitant. She silently concentrated drinking her brew.
Saumya looked at her expectantly!

"What happened? Is he alive?" She laughed at her own joke. Shakti laughed in unison.

"Very much alive madam!" She smiled again widely showing off her gutkha-smeared teeth from ear to ear.

"Then what? Some jaadu? (magic). Is he well?" She nudged on.

What Shakti told her changed her world. Shakti was the labour woman from a far off village in Andhra pradesh, with five children. The eldest being 10 and the next 8 and all the others in succession of two years were totally dependent on the money that she brought home. She had a man called her husband who brought not money but drunkenness, day in and day out every night. He was a Rickshaw driver and would slander money in gambling. After the days earnings were lost he would drink and return home to hit Shakti and eat up the food and go to sleep. The same story continued the next day. It was 11 years since her marriage that she suffered in the hands of this callous drunkard. The poor woman, on the other hand came home with the days supplies that generally consisted of some rice, lentils and oil to cook food for the 8 hungry people. That also comprised of her old mother in law who supported her by looking after the little ones while she was out laboring away the day. These people did not know dreams. They only knew hunger and hard work.

"I had returned from work madam as usual !" Shakti was recounting.
"Ok?"

"I had cooked some lentil and put a big utensil of rice to cook on the wooden stove. I was bone tired and worried as the kids were falling around asleep. In fact, the younger of the lot had already slept. My youngest one was running fever and I was very upset when my drunkard husband walked in with the demands of a grand dinner to be served to him immediately."

"Give me food, you useless woman." He screamed as usual.

"While this man had come in with demands. I said that the food was not ready. He started a ruckus."

"Then what happened?" Rejoined Saumya curiosity eating at her.

"Nothing I only requested him again while he pulled my hair hard. The sick baby in my lap started to howl."

"Naturally!" added Saumya."Then?"

"Even after an hour as I served everyone dinner, he did not want to eat lentil. He started to hit me hard. Somehow, I managed to get back into the kitchen."

She looked at the quizzical expression of Saumya.

"Madam we all eat in the front room."

Her maid lived in a makeshift house which was a part of deserted half constructed building in the slum. "The smaller children ate and slept immediately with the bigger ones. But the sick baby was still crying. My mother in law asked my husband not to create any problems as the child was sick. By then he started to fight with his mother also, idiotic man!"

Shakti hissed while Saumya smiled understandingly.

"Don't ask me madam that day was very bad. He was screaming at his mother and they both started to fight while I took the sick one with me into the kitchen."

"Oh...!" Saumya moved her head side to side in disgust.

"I tell you these idiotic men are sometimes ..." She stopped to think not knowing what to say."Idiotic!"She finally proclaimed.

 Her maid agreed.

"But what happened then? How did he change?"

Her maid was quiet for some time. 'The story had started only ten minutes back, but it was very engrossing. In-fact this is more interesting than any fiction!' Saumya thought sheepishly.

"Did he change because of the sick child or did he change later? What happened? Does he not beat you and scream at you at all?"

"No not at all. He is changed. He still drinks but he never comes near me or home angry!"

"What? What?"

"Yes madam, he does not do anything. He is changed now!"

 "Did he change that day?"
"Yes madam!" Her maid felt Saumya had a strangely guilty expression on her face.

"Is he alive?"

As a last resort Saumya asked again and laughed. They both laughed.

"Yes, yes madam." Shakti laughed.

"So, what?"

Shakti continued.

"He should not be that cruel na? Hitting me, pulling my hair and also fighting with his mother."

Shakti's most beautiful feature was her thick long knee length hair. Though she was dark, ugly plump and buxom.

Saumya smiled diligently and complemented her on her hair.

"Naturally he will pull your hair, that is the handiest one!" She observed tongue in cheek.

Shakti continued, "I wanted to keep the small one who was running high temperature with me. My husband joined me after sometime, into the kitchen and closed the door. He wanted to have sex that day. It was a deliberate thing to trouble me."

"Really!"

"I refused and again he started to fight and pull my hair. When the baby started to weep and cry the other children also woke. They started to bang on the door."

"Then?"

"He hit me very hard and threw the little one on the floor. Then something came over me madam!"

"Oh what?"

"Somehow I pulled my hair out of the hands of that drunkard. He started to hit me more. He punched my face. He kicked me in my abdomen. I fell on the ground next to the wooden choolah (heater). I started to bleed from my nose."

"Oh God! Then?"

It was like a thriller that Saumya could not wait to hear.

"Madam in the fit of the brawl I had to save my child and myself!"

"Yes?"

"My hands started feeling around for something while getting hit and kicked! Me and my baby were on the floor and my husband was standing over me! My child madam had fallen face down and screaming! Something came into my hands…!"

"Ok... What?"

"You know my husband is not very tall na… I just started to hit him on the legs with the hot wood. He started to scream and fell on the ground. The outside noises stopped on hearing their father screaming."

Saumya was incredulous. "You mean the firewood?"

"I stood over him as he fell down and started hitting him as much as I could. A couple of times he tried standing but he was too drunk. I just went on hitting him as much as I could. I realized that he was so drunk that he could not stand afterwards na?" Shakti asked and said at the same time.

Shakti was laughing at her own joke!

Saumya was laughing wide eyed.

"Then?"

"Nothing madam that day I was so angry that I went on hitting till he started to beg!"

"Oh!"

"I hit him like I got possessed and he started to beg

forgiveness saying that Devi ma please leave me, please leave, don't hit me anymore. Please, please! You are going to burn me." Shakti went on about it as it gave her an all-time jubilation.

"Did you stop?" Saumya laughed and laughed.

"No! I went on till he could not speak anymore. I asked him to leave me alone and the kids, when he was drunk. I told him "Khabardar (dare you) if you ever even touch me or any of my children!"

"Then?"

"He was begging, and I was hitting. He was begging and calling me kali ma leave me... kali ma leave me! Please forgive Kaali mata!"

"Oh God! Then?" Now Suamya was very quiet. She had tears in her eyes.

"I just wound my hair in a bun picked my sick baby and opened the door and walked off into the night and sat outside in the street breastfeeding."

"Oh God!" Saumya just fell into peels. "What was your husband doing then?"

"My husband was on the ground crying for forgiveness!"

"Oh that's awesome really. When you went out?"

"Yes madam! He was on the ground reeling with pain and asking for forgiveness. He was going on like- Mujhe maaf karo… maaf karo (please forgive me, please)! My wife has hit me, burned me." He cried for a long time and slept on the ground like a dead man!"

Saumya was totally reeling.

"What about the other people?"

"My mother-in-law was standing outside looking like a donkey for sometime madam. She went to sleep saying nothing."

"You must have really looked like a Kaali ma!" Saumya added laughing.

"Yes, madam my husband was calling me Kaali ma!"

"Witnessing their father on the floor begging for mercy my children fell on the mattress, pretending to sleep. Nobody said anything, including my neighbors thinking of it as one of our usual brawls." Shakti added.
"Oh?"

Saumya had stopped laughing by now.

"Haan, all children are very happy that the father

is not hitting me. He is changed. He still drinks but he is not shouting and hitting me. He gives some money in the house. He is eating whatever food I cook and sleeping peacefully."

"My God!"

"My people are thinking he has changed on his own."

After saying it she picked the cups and went into the kitchen.
Saumya called after Shakti for a second serving.

As Shakti came in with the poha, Saumya could not but look at the woman with admiration.

This woman was uneducated, poverty stricken but she had taught her a valuable lesson.

'Abusers were weak people!'

Saumya ate rest of the breakfast quietly. She learnt something great from someone she could never think she will.

The next two days flew fast. Raghav returned. Saumya had some time to think about what she wanted to do. She knew that her parents would be reluctant to take her back, but she had decided.

"You need not tell them everything." Her good friend Rathika advised wisely. "Let them know that you needed some time away from your spouse and tell them that you would go back after a few days. Assure them that there will be no problem for them. Give them a definitive return time to your home as well."

"Yes, that is a good idea." Saumya added. "I never thought of it possibly thinking Raghav would change."

"Dear, such people take a long time to change. Remember!"

Rathika added. "But still this is a temporary solution to your problem. If you really want to leave him then you need to think of a permanent solution."
Saumya nodded.

After his return, Raghav seemed to be nice. It was always the case.

"Darling I missed you badly."

"He is a very insecure guy!"
Rathika had said later as Saumya recalled how her verbally abusive spouse's behavior was so mushy, mushy after a gap.

As predicted, Raghav was himself after those initial

days. The same old ways returned back. The same stalking on the phone asking for explanations renewed!

It was a Saturday after he returned and Saumya had to sit late working as more clients dropped in for advises. Her usual half day got extended while her husband fumed sitting on the couch and watching T.V.

"Why are you late? You always like to sit around and have fun even if you do not have work. Having fun is what you want!"

Saumya was not stunned but taken by surprise surely.
She dropped the laptop bag on the bed and proceeded to the cupboard to change. But her fuming husband would not allow her to. He demanded an explanation again.

"Why are you so late?"

"I had work. You know when the clients come, we cannot leave them, need to work overtime. I have to work tomorrow half day. (Sunday was Saumya's weekly off on request while others worked) I need to go."

"Oh really? Now you need to work on Sundays too? Whom are you going to meet?" Raghav's words shook her.

"Who am I going to meet? I have work Raghav." In the days that he was away Saumya had changed. He noticed a streak of agitation and some confidence that took him by surprise. It was the first time that she had answered back in months.

"I am very tired besides I am hungry."

"Yes of course. Now that the queen is hungry, she will order food from out!"

"Did I say that?" Saumya cried out, all put together something had triggered inside her.

"I was going to cook but now I am so darn tired that I am not going to."
She cried. She was afraid of the consequences. She was weak compared to her towering spouse. She quickly thought. She needed to get out.

Something had split inside her suddenly. She had contemplated to leave but when? She was not clear. Now she was.

For some reason Raghav went away and started to work on his laptop in front of the T.V.

She grabbed her mobile and locked herself in the toilet. She was totally drained and had no inclination to cook or for that matter do anything. The sheer impact of fighting with her spouse after a hard days' work was too much. The very audacity to just relax while she toiled outside and inside the home was unbearable. It was not at all the kind of life that she had wanted for herself before marriage. On all their dates, Raghav had swept her off her feet totally. They were just cherished memories. She had never imagined that he was a demon in sweet demeanor.

He had never really touched her body, but he had created a shaft in her heart so deep that, it entered her soul uninterrupted.

"I want to break away!" She just said sobbing softly.

"Come over!" Was the silent yet full of strength reply from her friend.

"I will!" Rejoined Saumya quietly and walked out of the bathroom. She went on with her usual business of making chapatis.

As she served dinner that day she was mentally switched off. She silently prayed that the food on the table is accepted in peace! She had managed to fry the fish and put the last-minute touches to the Kali dal that her maid had prepared that morning. She silently prayed that the table ritual goes uneventful!

"The fish is fried a little too much!" Was the first

comment of her great spouse. "Why are you not responding? The fish and the dal have to be improvised."

"Ok."

"Ok? What do you mean?"

"I will see to it that nothing is missing next time!"

"Hmm. Can you pass the salt then?" He added the very next moment in an insulting tone.

She did.

After a couple of days as he prepared to leave for work, she hung around. Generally, she was ready and almost leaving on his footnote.

"What happened now…don't tell me that you are not going to work? I have to bear with your bickering and feed a useless person now? Don't tell me you are tired of your job and want to take a break? If you stay at home….?"

"No, no I am going a little late today."

"Late?"

"Yes! I am not well and besides the clients will come late."

"Thank God you did not say that "I have to go to the doc" and throw a fat bill on my face.""

Saumya squirmed. He had taken her to the councilor thousands of times after her first breakup and paid all the bills. That was before their marriage. That had got them together as she used to cling to him crying. At that point she thought of him as a man sent from Gods.

As her husband left and the maid finished her work, she kept things in a small brief, taking care not to leave her jewelry, certificates, some clothes, additional house keys, along with the marriage certificate. As she kept the papers in she faltered a bit, reading their names together.
'Married to Raghav Mehta' danced in front of her eyes. A wry smile crossed her face. She sighed as the pain seared in.

She looked, one more time around the house as she came to the entrance. She could not move. She went back slumped on the sofa taking in everything and finally broke down! April looked solemnly into her eyes feeling her pain. She decided to take April along.

She did not plan to go to her parents. She was going to Rathika's second home in Delhi. Staying in the same city was difficult for her. Besides, Raghav could find her. She planned to speak to her parents later.

Presently After four Years----

Saumya today is a free woman. Free from within and without. She is healed from the emotional wounds and knows that a physically abusive marriage can be battering but emotionally abusive relationships can be worse as they can, break one part by part till you are unrecognizable! Raghav was un-accepting and unrelenting but had no choice but to move on.

Today she has her own dog grooming parlor and devotes to the cause of rescuing helpless animals.

Alpesh was her client. He is more than that now! Her best friend, soulmate and someone who knows and understands her inside out!

She plans to start a family very soon even if the intent of marriage do not work out for her in the near future. Alpesh is her sound board. She goes back to an assuring smile and open arms after a hectic day with an undying anthem -

"I am always there for you."

❇ ❇ ❇

STORY - 4

Compassion

Narmada looked teary eyed around the bushes and the surroundings. Her feet dipped into the muddy sand soiling her ankles. The colonies near to the sea shore had this kind of a sand. Bushes and trees grew abundantly! She called out loud once more!

"Popsi!"

There was no reply.

Narmada walked a stretch of bushes that grew next to the sea. Here, the bushes were scanty and so were the trees. Humans had made a trail that she could see. She walked the trail and came up to a small deserted shack of a hutment.

"Popsi?"

She screamed. There was no reply. This was the second day she was searching for her one-year old Cavalier king Charles which was not fully grown to its maximum size.

It was a great looking black and white furry one, true to its breed it was a great tail wagger too. In fact, it could be traced from far because of its constant wagging that wagged its entire back body along.

Narmada could not see with eyes full of tears. It was the second day in a row and her dog was missing. There was no trace of her lovely pet and she had no food in the two days since it went untraced. She realized how close she felt to her wagging pet since it went missing.

"Popsi!" She cried out again in uneven tones with silence reverting back!

Her younger brother, mom and her papa took turns to search. Her friends searched along too. A couple of them joined that day in her endeavor after their school hours combing the underbrush adjacent to the shore. As for her she was at it whenever she could.

It was a Sunday the previous day, when Popsi just vanished. After a night of crying, Narmada was in no mood to go to school early morning. Her parents had let her be.

Now she called again with no response! Popsi was such a friendly trusting pet. Narmada's eyes welled again. She could not bear to think what could have happened to her four-legged friend, in the outside world? Horrendous ideas of trafficking, killing, treacherous handling, came to her mind. Narmada had watched a horrible video of how stray and abandoned dogs were put to rest. Worse was the way they were treated along the way.

She cried out, "Popsi come to mama!" She wept a bit walked along murmuring to herself.

"Where did you go? Mama cannot live without you! Cooome."
She was weepy, and the tears were unrelenting.

For the past one year, Popsi was with them, she knew only the neighborhood and the beach where she was taken for her long walks. Narmada had scanned the beach in its totality. A tear escaped creating a long trail as it went to the edge of her little jaw and stayed there precariously before falling to the ground. As more welled and flowed she went on relentlessly calling.

"Popsi?" Then an elongated call. "Poooopsiii?"

But she was not rewarded by either a tail wagging nor any sound of underbrush moving. Narmada craned to hear the kind of sound Popsi could make when she approached. The soft padded paws with nails swish sloshing on the wet sand. That was the kind of sound she was so used to.
Her Popsi would play games many a times hiding and jumping on to her master with a licking lolling tongue.

"Popsi!" The sound hardly escaped her this time, what with a throat constricted with mucus?

Narmada wanted to cry aloud. She looked around. She could see a couple of children in a distance searching for her pet. They were shouting the pet's name. The underbrush was thick at some places while it was less in some. All types of fearful thoughts came to her mind. Somebody suggested the pet might be injured and maybe lying in the bush.

Narmada for one could not visualize such a situation. She went on calling out to her dear Popsi. There was no response. After a continuous search for two hours she gave up. It was six in the evening and the sky was getting darker. She lived in a nearby building on the beach. She started walking towards it with a heavy heart!

She was joined by her two friends who were a part of her search team. On coming closer they signaled that they could not find him. Narmada's eyes brimmed again! Hot unstoppable tears rolled down wetting her already tear trailed cheeks.

Slowly the small group retraced homeward disappointed. While Narmada shed silent tears, the group walked. Her friends mumbled under their breath something un-intelligible from time to time.

The whole group was a bunch of early teen girls. Narmada was in her 8th grade and the others were in the 7th. Rathi's phone rang. Her mom was calling her back.

"Yes ma, I am on my way back ma." She answered.

The group trudged the extent of the beach to their buildings nearby. There were a few evening pet walkers. This was that part of the beach that was a little deserted. Scavengers and rag pickers came here in search of plastics, cans and bags.

Revathi spoke after a long gap.

"My cousin had lost his dog." The other two looked at her sharply. Narmada's eye brows came together.

"He lives in the U.S..." came her reply to the quizzical looks.

"Then?" The others asked together.

"He got it back after a week!"

"Oh!" Narmada sighed. "How? Did it wander home on its own? Or?"

"No, a neighbor found him."

"Oh!"

The group fell silent again.

"My cousin made flyers and circulated them in the neighborhood."

"Oh!" All said.

"With the dogs' pictures."

"Oh! I am worried my Popsi must be hungry for two days. I cannot eat as well. Feeling so sick!" Narmada started to cry once more. "Somebody must have taken her away or she might have been run over by a car!"
She wept.

"How did she get lost in the first place?" Rathi must have asked this question a hundredth time to her friend.

"We were all having lunch yesterday and the door was open. He was not on leash. He wandered off, I think. That is what my mom says. For an hour we thought that he was sleeping under the bed. His usual place. But by evening, when he did not emerge for his dinner from anywhere, I started calling out to him. Searched under the bed and not finding him, hunted through my home. After some time, when I could not find him, I felt…" she paused for breath, "Raised an alarm that Popsi was not visible." A tear dropped from the corner of her cry-worn red eyes.

"My papa, bro and others called out to him. There was no sign." She continued. "Towards late evening we realized that he was not in the house. We started to search in the neighborhood.

"Then?!"

"Nothing! I have lost my dear Popsi." Narmada said in uneven tones.

Both the girls held her. Supporting, they brought her to her building.

The buildings here were not sky scrapers. Hardly a three-story construction and the neighborhood was a one happy family amidst the cluster of 5 complexes next to Juhu beach. The cluster of these buildings were not on the main beach where the food stalls were erected but a little further down where there was no crowd and bustle.

Narmada reached home.

Some Hours Later------

Beautiful large brown eyes stared back at her. Narmada looked at the screen. The collection of photos was of Popsi.

The computer screen blurred as tears rolled silently. The night was dark and the whole family was sleeping. She woke up with a start at midnight and realized what disturbed her solely. She had walked on tip toes to the machine.

Her friend Revathi's words reverberated in her ears.

"My cousin had posted some flyers and one of the neighbors brought back their dog."

Narmada sneaked out of the bed, pulling off the bed clothes she gingerly climbed out, without disturbing her brother sleeping next to her. She did not bother switching the light on as it could wake the others. She left the bathroom light on after she stepped into the loo and left the door ajar for it to reflect enough into the room for her to see things around. She switched on the computer and went to the file where the family pictures were. There she found her Charles Cavalier Spaniel.

"Popsi…!" She cried in silence.

The long dropping ears, golden brown eyes, a white nose and a head that was spotted at places with black looked back.

"These Cavaliers are family dogs. That means that you cannot leave them alone at home or anywhere else." The owner had warned them when they had decided to bring this pup home.

More tears welled.

'My Popsi is somewhere out there alone! God alone knows how he must be coping?' She thought.

Her brother moved in his sleep. The light from

the bathroom fell on his cherubic face. He looked peaceful. He was equally disturbed. He cried intermittently remembering Popsi most part of the day.

From the moment he had returned from school he was morose. He also wanted to join the hunt party of Narmada and her friends, but their mom was not very open to the 7-year old joining, the girls team. Besides he was too young and an odd man out according to the lady of the house.

Presently he moved in his sleep. Narmada maneuvered the mouse carefully lest she might make sound and wake him.

At that instant she decided to design a flyer for her beloved dog.

She considered what should be the best way to make one so that she could get him back. She mentally made a check list.

'Something has to be written about Popsi. A catchy headline?'

The experience of writing reports for English projects came handy. A wry smile broke through sadness at the memory of her English teacher frantically shouting at them to perfect the headings and sub-headings for eye ball grabbing.

'I think all this information and a photo should be good for a flyer.' She nodded in a self-talk, self-assurance mode.

'Miss had taught me that headline should be catchy.' She mused sleepily. She never thought her merit winning reports would be practically helping so close to home one day.

Finally, she opened the pages and decided to type.

Selecting a close-up picture of Popsi, aligning into position to perfection, where it should, she decided- 'Over the photo I can write the header!'.

The innocent face of Popsi smiled back with the long ears and a protruding tongue.

Tears brimmed again as her little heart ached. She looked out. The regular night looked darker.

'In such a dark night where her Popsi must be?' Her body shuddered so as her heart pounded, in a panic attack.

Scary thoughts ran through her little head.
There was rustle behind her.

Her mom had woken up to peep in. She was standing behind, a sleepy yawn escaping her. A tender hand came on Narmada's back. Understandably, a speechless support.

She whispered, "What are you up to darling?"

"Making a flyer," came a quick whisper that sliced through the quiet.

Narmada had spoken almost to herself.

Her mom sat back on the bed and just reclined on her sleeping son after a while, Narmada pressed herself for a proper header for the flyer. At last she wrote,

MISSING! MISSING! MISSING!

The picture of Popsi large, clear, white and black with innocent button eyes, protruding tongue was aligned below it.

She continued typing:

'My Lovely Dog Popsi is missing since yesterday. It has black and white patches. It is very friendly and a one-year old Cavalier King Charles Spaniel. Pls. call

7746984734 if you find him.

We will wait for your call. Please call immediately as he is not at all used to living alone.'

Narmada added in her own worrisome, childlike language. She saved the flyer on the desktop. Sat staring at the screen for some time that had their family picture with the dog.

Next day Narmada walked to her school with Rathi and Revathi. The school was a ten minutes walking distance from her home. The small group of three were engrossed in their own thoughts. Rathi and Revathi looked at Narmada intermittently without talking much and Narmada's eyes scanned the landscape again and again.

'Who knows?' She told herself.

She did not say anything about it but everyone in the group knew that she was searching. After making the flyer the previous night she had not slept for a while though her mom had tucked her in. Finally, she had fallen into an exhausted disturbed sleep, dreams full of four-legged animals resembling dogs.

The road was wide and had large trees on either side. The ocean breeze waved the branches above and the children walked in groups to a nearby International school.

"I have made a flyer!"

The other two girls looked at Narmada as she suddenly exclaimed.

"Oh!"

"I am going to distribute it in the neighborhood after school."

"You have to stick on the trees as well." Rathi added. "That way everyone can see. My cousin in the U.S had done it. That is how they got their dog back!"

"Ok, will you guys…" As Narmada had started to talk the other two girls rejoined in unison,

"We will come to your place at 2 after school today and we will take the flyers out to stick on the trees and shops after lunch. We were planning yesterday to come too, to visit you."

"Ok. I will ask my mama also!" said Narmada. They neared the school and once all the three reached the gate, they ran to their respective classes. While Narmada was almost 13 the other two were little younger to her. Rathi was 12 and Revathi was almost there. But both studied in the 7th C while Narmada was in 8th D class. However, all the classrooms were on the same floor.

They all walked out at the same time for the assembly after keeping their bags safely in the rooms. They again joined in the corridor. As they forked out into their respective class rows; bade a silent good bye for the time being signaling to each other to meet at Narmada's house later.

The school seemed to drag that day. Every minute Narmada thought of her Popsi. When she opened her tiffin to have her chapati role she could not but wonder what her Popsi must be doing. She finally kept the role back and pushed the box away. Her class teacher on noticing patted her concerned.

"What happened? Don't you like what you got today?" She tried to sound cheerful though, she knew that something was awfully amiss about her student Narmada.

Some girls around her looked her way. They were in a close group, eating away their snacks.

"She has lost her puppy!" One girl in piggy tails exclaimed.
Though they had all come to the standard 8th, they were still very kiddish.

Most of them had not lost their cherubic looks.

Miss Alissa their beautiful young teacher in her late twenties nodded sadly.

"When did she go missing?"

"Sunday. It's a he." Narmada added almost weepy.

"Oh! I understand how you feel. I know because I had gone through it myself as a child."

"Did your pet come back home ma'am?" The girl sitting next to Narmada asked.

The teacher did not say anything. That was cause enough for more sadness for Narmada. She understood the unspoken answer. Miss Alissa coaxed Narmada to bite into a couple of pieces from her roll. The break went off slowly and the rest of the classes crawled through the day.

It was two in the afternoon when Narmada reached home. Her lunch was again a few meagre morsels thrown in.

She sat at the comp looking at the various pictures of Popsi and simultaneously gave a print order to her machine for 20 copies of the flyer. After printing she looked at the paper. There the open mouthed Popsi stared back again.

Tears welled deep into Narmada's eyes again. She was a scene to behold. For three days she had not slept nor eaten well. Every moment of her life was filled with her four-legged friend.

"Let's paste the pictures near to the market and the D'Mart." Her friend called to say.

"You guys were going to be here at 2, it's almost 3?" Narmada wailed.

"Yes. We will be. I am waiting for Revathi!"

Exclaimed Rathi.

Narmada did not speak much.

Her mom came in and went out. Her bro had not yet come home from school.

Mrs. Amrita Ranjan Narmada's mom was worried for her daughter more than the dog.

"Are you going to paste the flyers today darling?" Her mom asked in the sweetest of the voices.

"Yes ma…" Narmada said in a small pitch.

"How far would you be going?"

"The entire neighborhood ma!"

"Umm! Be careful. Don't go very far beta!"

"But…" Narmada raised her voice to complain, "If I do not paste the flyers everywhere how am I going to find my brother." Brother as in Mrs. Amrita realized Popsi.

"Don't worry! I mean don't go very far don't drift unmindfully. Please call and inform where you have gone in case?"

"Ok ma!"

Narmada just muttered under her breath.

Her friends arrived at 3 in the afternoon.

All of them ventured out along with some 20 printed pamphlets, a small bottle of adhesive and some pinup board pins. It was the brain wave of Rathi who thought that if the paper did not stick it could be pinned up to a tree bark instead.

The small group walked through the lane after stepping out of the building. They stuck a couple of posters on a nearby tree in the lane where Narmada lived. There were a lot of trees lined up on either side of the road. "Mom said not to waste the posters." Narmada informed the group, about her mother's advice.

Both girls nodded.

They applied the gum with the small brush and stuck the posters randomly leaving a few trees in-between.

"I think all the trees are covered." Rathi announced after a while. They had come to the end of their lane.

"Hey you know what? We should stick a few near to the D'Mart. There people come and go; there is a big crowd every evening." Revathi advised. All three nodded without a word.

They sauntered towards the mart.

Slowly walking, Narmada chatted with her friends. At the back of her mind always worrying about what she had lately.

'How he must be? Where he must be?'

Tears threatened to trip over miraculously remaining inside the lids, an astonishing feat she could master in the days that followed the unforeseen loss! Her small chest heaved too now and then twinning in support of the grief!

They reached D'Mart after a while.

They started pasting the flyers on some lamp posts near to the mart.

As they stuck five to six the group felt satisfied. They decided to return homeward.

"I think it's enough for today. Hope to get some feedback." Narmada muttered under her breath.

She stood a while looking at the poster from little afar, her face twisted at an angle to grab its feel. Her dog's tongue lolling picture tugged at her. A tear that was threatening, finally dropped. Her friends put a hand each from either side.

After a while, they all walked slowly back.
The posters receded farther and farther till they disappeared altogether.

The group finally reached Narmada's building. Rathi and Revathi bade goodbye.

"Will meet you in school tomorrow."

Narmada nodded. Tears did not stop now. She cried for some time into the comforting arms of her friends.

Finally, as she stopped crying, they accompanied her all the way to the lift and as Narmada went up to her flat, the two friends waved and retraced.

Days passed, and the time went by. Narmada waited for that one phone call that would change it all. Nothing happened. She dragged herself, day in and day out to the school and back home; cried buckets when she remembered her dear dog. After weeks and weeks of consoling and prayers she could resume 'a near normal demeanor', otherwise everything about Popsi made her cry. Her family stood by her. Her brother mourned the loss too. He would remember little things Popsi did or felt. As life goes on so did the lives of the two children of the Ranjan family did.

"When we got a pet home, we did not realize it would become a part of the family, a sibling to the kids." Mrs. Ranjan would exclaim to her neighbors.

The greatest blow of course Narmada endured.

Her grief was unbound, and her little heart could not explain the loss that she felt every moment, for Popsi was like a sibling.

Days passed so did the months. Parents told Narmada to get one more dog, but she was adamant. To speak the truth Mrs. Amrita was not sure she wanted to keep one more pet. The loss was too much besides she realized her children were devastated at the untoward happening.

The teachers in school spoke highly about keeping pets for the emotional development in young children because of which the Ranjan's had got their dog.

Invariably Deep's (Narmada's Brother) English lesson of fifth standard praised how pets were a blessing to a family with young children.

Inadvertently, Deep would remember Popsi and feel sad every time he read the chapter.

Deep's term needed a practical service for social causes of 20 marks in that semester and he opted to volunteer for helping underprivileged children with disabilities in the slums of Mumbai. For that he had to visit the nearby slums and study the conditions of such kids in the neighborhood.

He along with 14 other children was assigned to

one of the Mumbai hospitals in the slum, that had a training and care unit for underprivileged children with disabilities. These normal kids would visit and study the conditions and if possible, would provide help. That was one of the major social work responsibilities for Deep's class along with some orphanages that were assigned to the school for social awareness work.

Deep took leave of his mom that Friday to go Visit the nearby Govt. hospital that had a training and care unit for children with disabilities. This was an optional class for students. The others who had not opted for social work went for nature trail excursions and wrote about environment after school.

"Ma, I will be late. My class has the social work assignment today. I will be going to Jeevan Jyot Govt hospital in Dabar Nagar nearby."

"Is your class teacher with you? How will you go?" His mom enquired as usual concerned.

"Yes…we will visit in the bus."

"Oh! OK. But please keep to the group and don't venture far from the other kids and the teachers. Is it Sonali ma'am who will accompany you guys?"

"Yes ma!'

"Ok I will call her and ask about the bus number."

Mrs. Ranjan had the numbers of all the cleaners and bus drivers of Deep's school including his class teacher Sonali.

Deep nodded reluctantly. He hated his mom calling the drivers and teachers of his school. But he had no choice!

After the school was over that day, the children of each class were divided according to their assignments to a particular social work segment. They were 15 of them in each group with a teacher, driver, a maid and a cleaner. The mini buses took the children on these small excursions.

After a while, settling into the bus the kids ate their small snacks that they got from home as the bus slowly chugged through the lanes of the neighborhood.

Deep went on to eat his cheese sandwich his many favorites from the home tiffin box packed by his mom lovingly in the morning. This was an usual snack for his small school social activities. Along with the bigger meal she would provide a smaller box, generally comprising his favorite snack.

He munched on the sandwich savoring the taste simultaneously keeping an eye out at the passing views. He enjoyed the bustling roads and the moving traffic. He noticed slum children playing on the sidewalks next to their huts in abandon. The stray dogs ran along the playing kids enjoying their pranks.

"Dogs are man's best friends." Teacher had said it in the class. His face fell at the thought.

The whole by lanes had a festive feel of playfulness with the children and dogs and hutments of women and men just lying around or busy in their daily afternoon chores.

Deep remembered how Popsi used to play and tug along their clothes while he was with the other kids in his locality.

"Children with special needs, focus at the world around them in ways that might vastly differ from our own perception. That does not mean there is anything wrong with them. These children have a unique perspective to life that causes them to experience things differently. I can say, in their own way."

The teacher was explaining as a running commentary to the kids. Deep was absent minded most part of it and almost dozed through the talk. Every time his eyes closed his teacher's voice faded into the background. He would be jolted back again and would concentrate on what she had to say. He paid attention more out of fear than interest.

"It is our job as normal responsible individuals to understand a special child rather than forcing them to follow us." The teacher emphasized.

Deep nodded sleepily. He understood perfectly as a fifth grader that they needed to be more pro-active individuals, specifically towards the society. He was a bright boy and he looked forward to these outings with his classmates.

"We need to be more thankful to our parents for providing us with these great opportunities." The teacher exhorted.

All children responded in chorus that they were.

"Yes Ma'am."

"And also, be thankful to God almighty that we have been blessed with the perfect faculties that we have." She continued.

"The children with special needs, face many struggles on a daily basis."

As the destination neared their teacher instructed, "Now all the kids present here will align out of the bus in a line one after the other without pushing or pulling?" She almost shouted.

"There are additional marks for perfect behavior and discipline, mind you!"

The children became restless as the bus neared a huge gate that housed a school for special children.

As it took a turn in front of the building, Prateek who was sitting next to Deep nudged him with his sharp elbow.

Deep gave him a 'dare you' look and stood up to align with the kids queued up to leave. Prateek followed suit but fell on him. Hassled, Deep again looked angrily into the fat kids eyes.

Warning signs emitting out of each other, Prateek and Deep jumped out of the bus and fell into place with the queue. The teacher stood with vigilant looks while the maid in charge counted the boys and girls along including the cleaner. The teacher finally nodded approval at the maid's signal of satisfaction.

Sonali ma'am requested the group to continue. She shouted.

"Follow me into the school. Remember that these kids are very special and much younger to you. Today we are going to meet the first graders. What you need to do is, walk into the class and sit on the chairs allocated to you. Observe and come back after half an hour. Ok? Mind you, nobody will misbehave. You can take notes." She concluded. Some girls chuckled.

"Do you want to write something?" One girl asked the other in front of her who obviously seemed to be in her afternoon snooze mode.

The listening girl just made a sound conveying negative.

However, teacher's tone meant business. Nobody dared to go out of the way to disobey. While some still mischievously nudged each other on the sly, others just obeyed orders, while some remained in their own world.

Prateek pushed at the kids behind him and before him too. Deep did not want to be a target of teacher's wrath, so he maintained as much distance as possible from the trouble makers.

A girl looked back towards Deep from the farthest beginning of the queue. She was Priyanka. She smiled at him. He smirked back. Every time Priyanka smiled at Deep, he felt obliged to do something for the girl. She was the topper of the class and both had a huge crush on each other. Only that, they did not know about it as 5th graders, they were just at the helm of teenage hormonal histrionics.

Both Priyanka and Deep exchanged glances now. Priyanka signaled to him that signified something to both of them. They had decided much in advance to sit together during the observation. Now, anxiety gnawed at them as they were separated.

Deep gave her a thumbs up, as they entered the building. The queue followed the teacher to the right of the corridor. At the end of it was a bright class room. A middle-aged man and a young lady were waiting for them, as the group with Sonali teacher and the maids arrived. The man put a finger to his lips signaling them to be quiet.

There ensued a slight scramble as the children were directed to the left end of a colorfully painted room to their chairs.

Deep tried to look around for Priyanka. As children took their seats Deep saw Priyanka occupying a chair and she had her hand on the one next to her. He ran towards it. In the process he stepped on Harshal's foot. She almost screamed, and the little clamor did not go unnoticed by the teacher. She quietened as the teacher's stern glance followed.

They had not distracted the other kids though, of the original class, busy with activities. There were around 20 deaf children. Deep and Priyanka sat hand in hand and Harshal grumped under her breath now and then. Finally, the class settled. They were ready for the observation study.

Now, children seemed to concentrate on the group in front of them. Deep concentrated too. The special educationist addressed them in sober tones.

"Everyone has a different way of relaxing. You might like to listen to music and read, some like to watch television?"

The children nodded.

"But for a child with special needs relaxation might be harder which is why a pet is used as a therapy. Animals work magic in this case without a special child ever knowing it." The teacher explained to the curious 5th standard.

Deep and Priyanka exchanged glances. 'Animals?' They mentally exclaimed.

Their glance that moment fell on a few dogs present in the class for the first time. The excitement was palpable. Deep felt butterflies in his tummy at the sight. The reason he could not see these friendly creatures before was because, the kids had surrounded them.

The special children with the needs were divided into a group of five each, with a dog and they were petting and playing with the furry four-legged creatures that looked every bit happy in their company!

Deep felt his heart beat faster!

The children moved their palms over the creatures and seemed to be meditating in their own quite world.

They seemed at peace like little personifications of Buddha. Some signaled to each other excitement taking over intermittently. The presence of these pets made the whole atmosphere stress free.

The teacher was explaining, "Dogs and horses are used for therapy. They can be domesticated and tamed and they are naturally friendly, trusting and thus loving."

Deep whispered, "I am missing my Popsi."

Priyanka nodded. Her face fell.

"Unconditional love of dogs develop natural love, trust and confidence in children with special needs. The child can teach the animals basic commands and as the dogs listen, that develops the power of communication with confidence, in a child." The teacher explained further.

'True, I am a confident child because of Popsi.' Thought Deep in his own childlike way.

The teachers asked them to take a round of the therapy going on at the end of their session before retreating into the bus. They all nodded quietly. The observing children enjoyed the sight of , special kids as they fondled and played with the cute dogs. There were five to six that roamed from group to group, child-to-child and enjoyed licking them, cuddling close, reveling in the fondling of the kids without getting agitated.

"They are trained dogs. One of them we got into the class very recently. He seems to be the friendliest around kids. He is the best so far in spite of being new." The teacher pointed to the farthest dog in the class that Deep's eyes had missed in the little crowd. He looked in the direction and froze. There in the corner he was, fondling and licking the kids and mocking them to follow. 'Was he? Was he not!' Deep's eyes tried focusing.

The same white wagging tail and the black nuzzle that prompted the kids to touch him. He teased them with his nose and set himself back on all fours. One moment gentle, next agile.

Without his own volition Deep found himself call.

"Popsi!" A stunned silence followed.

The whole class froze on the name. Even the special kids stopped their play as they sensed the astonishing vibe. It was the greatest and the deepest heart wrenching painful cry for affirmation.

"Popsi!"

Sonali and the special educator looked with a mixture of stern curiosity at Deep.

The dog turned in the direction of the sound. For a few seconds he froze as the watery brown eyes focused in recognition of what it solicited.

In the days and months that followed its separation it had walked the streets to hear this name, but in vain. Through hunger, desolation and traffic of death, it wanted to hear that name to go home. Only, it did not know; that it had strayed some long, long distance away from its loved ones. That he had come to another part of the city altogether.

Eventually, he was knocked by a speeding bike while crossing streets in a confused frenzy only after, a couple of days of its loitering astray.

When he opened his eyes, he met kind people and found himself in an animal shelter far, far away in another town on the highway, near to Mumbai. His extremely friendly nature around humans found him a place in the towns' top trainers. Finally, he was brought to the animal shelter for dogs that trained for special children! All the months, he was amongst kids, he wanted to see two faces- Deep and Narmada!

He was not Popsi now. He was Brandy. He realized his name had changed. But he had not forgotten his masters. How could he? After all he was still searching?

"Popsi!" came one more call and he had no doubt.

Deep was oblivious to the whole class. What happened next was what nobody ever imagined. Popsi jumped into Deep's lap and both had a session full of tears with deepest gurgles of happiness and whimpers.

"I had lost him! I had lost him! Where were you lost Popsi?" Deep tried explaining between his cries of happiness to the stunned teachers and children. "I am taking you home. Taking you home! Popsi. Love you! Love you! Taking you home!" He was rewarded next with the licks of a lifetime. The wagging did not stop either.

"Where were you? How have you been?" He could not say anything anymore as he had started to weep. Priyanka hugged him and Popsi together!

"That is Popsi. Deep's Dog! He searched for a long time but could not find him." Priyanka tried to pitch in to the stunned crowd.

Present Day.

Even though Deep took Popsi home he is brought to the special school regularly. As he is now a highly trained therapy dog. Popsi enjoys the best of both worlds. He has a special bond with the family and the kids in the school too. He can play to his heart's content with his favorite subjects--- CHILDREN.

❋ ❋ ❋

STORY - 5

Devotion

Priya stood at the entrance. The broad wooden door opened, and she walked in.

Today was the board interview. She had to face the committee for the final round. It was the officer's training academy, Chennai where she was facing the final council.

There were at least ten people in the room. All the commanding officers asked her to take a seat. She sat in the chair placed in front of the table. One commander had some papers, and another was gleaning through her academic track records that she had couriered and mailed to the panel a few days back. One general was gleaning at the computer at her documents while the other had a file in hand, of the printed version of the same. They were informed about her and well versed in her achievements.

"You are a Chemical engineer?" Captain Pant who was seated facing her enquired.

"Yes! She is a Chemical engineer with a post-graduation in Physics." Added Commander Robert Sapiens.

"Impressive!" said another.

"She has been a working lady for some time." Added Captain Arora.
Priya nodded.

"Impressive!" came in a chorus.

"We would however like to know your change of mind for joining the Indian army?"

"I was not sure initially." Priya started in small tone but clearly. "As Captain Arora called me six months back enquiring about it…" the gentlemen looked at her questioningly. Robert leaned forward.

Priya realized that she was not audible enough. She continued louder next.

"As I got a call from Captain Arora, I was not very sure. But as the days passed…" she paused, and the inquisitive panel nodded affirmative with curiosity.

"As the days passed, I just decided. I told myself why not? The only way I could serve my husband was to serve the forces he did."

The Panel was very quiet and listened attentively as Priya completed. They looked at her for more. But she had finished. She fell silent.

"That is a very good decision really. Welcome to the Indian army as a commissioned officer. We are happy to welcome you amidst us." Piped in the only lady officer from the cadet, Major Rajni Pattavi. Priya could read the labels on their uniforms and the colors and stars were many and marvelous. She was new to all this but not very new as her husband was with the army till last year.

Commander Rajni handed over her a sealed envelope.

"We have your medical reports and they are clear. Your academic records are very satisfying as well. As you are a technical grad you could appear for the interview directly. Welcome to the Indian army!" She repeated.

"It is sad that we are welcoming you this way but hope you are happy to serve our nation and it's a proud moment for all who join the forces in all forms. It's a great field and we learn a lot and hope it is also fruitful to you in every way." Added commander Rastogi from the far-off right end.

"This Short Service Commission, gives you the option of joining the Indian Army and serving it as a Commissioned Officer for 5 years. Once your tenure is over, you are allowed to opt for a Permanent Commission." Colonel Arun Agrawal added who was a commandeering officer of the forces.
Priya realized that the officers present in the chamber were all from different fields in different ranks of hierarchy. She nodded. There was a kind of disciplined silence in the room that could be cut through after the talking stopped.

"Alternatively, you can also choose for a 5-year

extension and can choose to resign from your post any time during this period." He added. By now the panel had very 'soft stern' expressions. That Priya would register very soon that came with the occupation.

"With a Short Service Commission, you will have the best of both worlds." added Commander Rajni again to reinstate the statements of Tadhani.

Priya nodded again. She had nothing else to do but to obey the orders of course. As the interview was just a formality according to the rules prescribed by the Govt of India she knew that she was going to serve the army for a long time. She was emotionally very attached to it. The formal interview was over. The head of the committee Colonel Viraj Solanki dismissed with a slight wave.

All stood as he did and Priya followed suit. Each one of them shook hands with her according to the hierarchy again.

'I need to get used to this professional scale', she told herself with a smirk that was invisible.
She walked slowly out of the room first allowing the committee members to do so.

They got engaged in small talk, while they were at it, major Rajni patted Priya on the shoulder. 'Being a woman has many advantages.' Priya thought. In this world of manly dryness, a woman brings in fresh touch of care. As if the lady major read her mind she seconded as they slowly made their way out.

"Priya, being a woman has many advantages. We bring in a lot of balance in the world where there is only conquest and power. We as women always bring in a breath of life and a touch of care!" Priya smiled again; her weak and indulgent smile.

"I agree ma'am. I feel a woman is complete in many respects. She is the one who teaches care and love to a man." She added.

Major Rajni smiled broadly. She understood perfectly from where Priya was coming. She had been a home maker for major part of her life and before to that a protected daughter. Now, as a mother and a home bound woman she had a limited vista of perception about the work places and let alone of the army. Major Rajni took note of the rough hands of the young woman used to tending home fires. She recognized a hibernating, yet to be liberated woman in front of her. She saw a reflection of herself in Priya. She patted once more on her shoulder and took leave quietly.
Priya walked the rest of the corridor alone. She left the building and outside the academy, she saw her brother waiting to take her home. He was seated on the parked bike checking his cell phone, not noticing her approach.

"Bhaiya?" Her voice was more of a question than a request.

"Hi, Arey! Sorry did not see you coming!"

"Ya,ok."

He looked at her questioningly.

"It went off well. They gave me this letter." Priya added showing the letter to Arun.

"Ok. Is it an offer?" Priya nodded. "Did they give you a date of joining?"

"Yes, from the first of next month."

"Ok!"

On that note, Priya hopped on to the bike behind her brother. They zoomed past the army training centre buildings and checked out of the main gate.
They fell silent for the rest of the journey to her home. In the normal circumstances it would have been a wonderful opportunity and a happy occasion but not now.
Priya aligned from the bike and walked the stone path to home. She lived in the army quarters that her husband worked for with her little daughter. The quarters were small segregated buildings away from town as all army colonies are. Each building had a gate and a couple of floors above the ground.

Priya lived in a small flat on the ground floor of 'H' block. All the buildings were demarcated as blocks after the alphabets categorically. Priya's brother waited till she opened the main door with her keys and walked in. She waved at him from one of the front windows and he sped away.

After bidding him good bye she just dropped herself on a sofa near to the aperture. She stayed there for some time looking around and not knowing what to do as the desolate house stared back. There were a lot of tasks around to be completed. The household things were just strewn around. They had to be put in place. She had no stamina whatsoever. Looking at the time in the clock alerted her. It was 1 in the afternoon and her daughter would be home by three. That gave her a couple of hours to keep things in order. Her mind raced to the kitchen.

She was happy she had completed the major cooking for the day. Her brother had mentioned about coming back in the evening for dinner. He lived in the small town of Madurai. He was a bank employee and it was transfer to a rural town in his service life. His wife and ten-year old son lived in Delhi where his spouse worked as an H.R manager and the boy went to an international school.

Priya sighed. In the 7 years of marriage to her husband she had seen a lot of life and problems closely. Both her in-laws and parents were no more.

She had her brothers' support now. She was married off when she was just 19 and since then she was just a housewife. The thought of going to work had not occurred to her at all. Her spouse however had encouraged her to study further and she went on to complete her post-graduation in Physics with flying colors. A tear escaped from her eye. Everything made her cry in the beginning. Even innocent gestures from her child reminded her of Ravi.

Practically anything and everything was a cause for her to fall into the pit for grieving. Almost a year had passed. She was less weepy and more normal now. The reason for her to brim above the painful incident was her little Pinky. In fact, she was the entire reason for her to look at life with a new meaning.

She vividly remembered the day. Priya's future looked nothing but bleak when she first heard the news. Ravi serving with the 13 Rajput regiment in a counter-insurgency operation near hilly Tawang in Arunachal Pradesh in 2010 had lost his life. He was serving in Colonel Arun Agarwal's unit. While others suffered injuries, he was no more.

When Colonel Arun Agarwal learnt Ravi had encouraged her to complete her degree in Chemical engineering and then PG, he thought she should become an officer. That was how things had moved for her.

Her brother initially refused to respond to the enquiries from the army about Priya joining it as the entire family was in shock. But later as the days passed and Priya sobered, she decided as to what could be a better way to serve her husband's memory but through army?

The whole process of induction into the job, did not take long as she had expected. She was put in the category of Direct Interview- through the service selection board. On the 1st day- Document Verification happened and on the 2nd - Screening, third step was the personal interview. She had expected a lot of questions but as it went that day the panel was very chilled out. She was not teamed up with others either. That was also because there were no women widows appearing for interviews. Intelligence tests and the psychological assessment were an option for her as per the screening for the short-term officers in the army. Since her husband died on duty and her qualifications fitted the bill the best, she was exempted from the lengthy procedures. She was selected solely by the technical graduation degrees.

Priya sighed and moved in the house aimlessly. She contemplated the obligations to her job, that might require her to travel a lot. She turned in her mind the possibilities of her little daughter adapting to the new environment again and again. A sigh escaped her.
"When the bridge comes, I shall cross it!" She

murmured to herself.

After Six Months....

Six months into the office, Priya seemed to adapt to her surroundings. She got curious glances from fellow men, but she learnt to hold it on her own during the meetings and conversations. One day as she walked into her cabin there was an envelope waiting for her on the table. She opened it to read about the press conferences for the lady officers of the army. She wondered what it could be.

Later, she realized that there was a special coverage in a particular national newspaper on Army female recruits. So, the press was coming to interview her and the others. They would be asking her few questions in the cabin itself. She had no clue whatsoever, but she was vaguely exited and looking forward to it.

She being the chemical engineer was posted to look after the Pharmaceutical department of the army that was responsible mainly to the tending of the fodder for cattle. The cattle supplied diary produce to the forces. She had learnt three key words in performing her duties. "Command, Control and Administration"

A couple of journalists were from one of the leading newspapers. They shook hands with her the moment they walked in.

"I am Avinash Mehra....Z News"

"I am Manjari Naik from the Times."

"Thanks for choosing me." Priya gestured them to take seats.

"There was no choosing you ma'am, you were in our recommended list. You were one of the first and the outstanding lady officers who joined the army to serve after her husband." Manjari said the last line little low as she was scared, she might trample on some unwanted emotions.

"Ma'am we will be asking you the regular questions. Though we know why you are serving the army, but still our readers need to know the details of a journey that could inspire them! Hope you are comfortable?"

Manjari adjusted her dicta phone to record the interview while Avinash readied his pen and the note pad to jot down.

"Since how long have you been here in the forces?" Avinash joined the conversation with a question.

"Six months! Almost." Priya rejoined.

Both young journalists in their twenties looked at

her and at each other. May be, they expected more or were thinking about how to frame the next obvious question. Manjari came to Avinash's rescue.

"What was your journey like while joining the forces?" It was a softer version of- "What made you join the army?"

Manjari and Avinash waited with bated breath. A delicate topic, the fear of hurting Priya was topmost on their minds.
Priya's response was smooth surprising herself.

"I had lost my husband Ravi serving with the 13 Rajput regiment in a counter-insurgency operation near hilly Tawang in Arunachal Pradesh in 2010." She paused while both the journalists breathed slowly in that spot less silence. They dare not look elsewhere since it was such a delicate subject. Priya continued.

"My brother received a call one day last year from Colonel Arun Agrawal, he had heard about my qualifications." The journalists looked at her sharply. Noting at the enquiring look Priya added.

"I am a chemical engineer." Both listeners nodded again.

"When Colonel connected with my brother, he was reluctant in the beginning as I was grieving and had no intention of living life as before. But as the days and months went by and I became better and understood that life had a bigger purpose, I had to live for my child if nothing. I just thought that what a better way to serve the nation than to join the forces that my husband worked in and gave his life for?"

Both young people agreed. They gave Priya a weak smile. Manjari could connect with otherwise delicate officer in front of her.

'Only a woman can understand another!'

She reasoned in her heart. She missed her boyfriend with whom she had broken up very recently.

"When I joined, I had no idea what life would be like. I had seen my husband and neighbors go to work every day for seven years. So the fascination with the blue uniform was my inspiration." She tried joking through the cracking voice.

Both people in the front nodded with respect. "These five plus years of numerous postings, meeting so many faujis and civilians, traveling through the length and breadth of the country are the definite highlights of being the wife of an army officer." Priya paused for breath.

"I guess I took the best decision of my life by joining as a licensing officer in the forces to serve my motherland. I feel proud and blessed."

"That is very nice to know, and I must say very inspiring as well." Avinash rejoined to ask. "What is the nature of work that you do as a chemical engineer?"

Priya paused for some time. "As a chemical engineer I am responsible for the chemicals used in the crops and the fodder that goes to the cattle that supplies milk for the army. I look into the right quantities of chemicals responsible for the growing of crops that are maintained by the army too. The dried-out maize, grass from the fields and the cut-out crops then become fodder for cattle."

Both the journalists nodded. Since Priya was not a very senior member of the force they had fixed less questions for her than the other officers.

"What work ethics you need to follow on a day to day basis?"
"Command, Control and Administration." Pat came the answer.

"These are the three golden rules of a successful execution of duties at my position. At least that is what I have learnt right now in this short term of my functioning here. I believe this works the best!"

"Ma'am could you please expand on the three key words that you first explained?"

Priya nodded.

"I reasoned that nobody will ever listen to you if you are not confident. The first drawback here could be that I am a woman. So first, I learnt to command. Command means execution of duties with confidence. Control would be supervising the said tasks entrusted to the people around. Administration is sum total of everything. Proper communication, supervising and ability to win the confidence of the subordinates."

"Wow well said." Reiterated Avinash while Manjari added.

"Words of inspiration for the young women and men of our country!"

Priya nodded again. "Actually, it is easier saying than doing. Every day is a horrendous task for me. I have learnt these golden rules by trial and error!" Concluded she in the end. Both the journalists nodded in agreement.

"We are also learning by trial and error. Each day we are illuminated by meeting inspiring people like you!"added Manjari seconding on to what Priya said.

After that, both of them left with a wave of the hand and the words, "We will be able to publish this inspirational interview with the Sunday edition ma'am."

Priya just reclined back in her revolving chair reminiscing the fruitful days with the army. That day was over, and an inspirational story was canned in by the press about an Indian army wife who could encourage other of her kind.

STORY - 6

Deceit

Nilesh heard the phone ring. He waited with bated breath. This was the tenth or the eleventh time that he must have tried. She was still not taking it.

"Hello?" Said a husky voice after a while. He jumped with happiness.

"I want to speak with Sudha." He blurted out immediately and held his breath.
"Why? She is sleeping." The woman answered rudely.
"It is urgent!"
"But she is sleeping."
"It's urgent!" He repeated.
"I cannot wake her up!"
"I know but..but?"

The phone went dead.

After the abrupt interruption, there was no reason for him to call again.
He could not agree more. It was only 7 in the morning and he knew that, his girlfriend slept late.

He decided to wait for the day to catch up in that part of the world.
He slowly went out of the booth and walked towards his apartment. It was Christmas time in New York and the weather was icy cold.

The sun had set but the down town was a beehive

of activities. Festive fervor was in the air. Everybody seemed to go somewhere. Vehicles sped past. Families flocked the stores, there seemed to be happiness everywhere. Except in his heart!

He pulled his hood over his head and walked with his legs closer. He needed all the warmth that he could sum around him. Through the pants, thermos and all the warm layers he wore the wintery chill made its way to the bones.
As the bones and body chilled the warm water inside his eyes welled. He was lost in thoughts and shook his head in disgust.

A vehicle crossed honking as the irate youngsters shouted from within.

"Where man? Look where you are walking?"

He waved at the youngsters absently as the hot liquid blurred his vision, he moped with the back of his hand to swipe clean. He felt icicles where there could have been liquid. The weather was definitely cold, and snow had started to fall steadily.

He could not do much from where he was. He had to just wait for the Sun to rise in India more.
Besides, the number was unknown to Sudha. He very much doubted if she would take the call since she did not entertain unknown numbers.

The icicles kept forming as he kept walking. The Hot

liquid transformed as it flowed down.

He trudged towards his apartment near Times square. He waited patiently for a few cars to pass. The drivers looked at him and the lights at the junction. It was clearly not the pedestrian crossing signal. He had ventured far into the lane without being mindful. He made through the other half of the street and stood under the lamp post close to his apartment, hands in the huge parka pockets and hood over his head.

After a while of standing there he decided to go up the street for a smoke. There was a general store run by an Indian sardar(Turbaned sikh) around the corner. The bells on the door chimed as he walked in.

He closed the door and stood there relishing the warmth for a few seconds. The Indian gentleman ushered him in.

"Namaste Saheb. Good evening!"
"Good evening" Chipped Nilesh.
"How are you sir?"

The hefty sardar enquired. In response Nilesh just nodded.

Sardar looked at him with a smile and went about his work as usual around the counter, calculating on the computer screen while Nilesh walked to his usual shelf, where the cigarettes were and pulled out a couple of packs.

His eyes fell on bear cans. He was lucky to find Kingfisher, his favorite brand. This was available only in some select Indian stores. More popular amongst the Indians, of course. He walked to the counter slowly taking into stock some of the available drinks. Picked none except kingfisher. He paid the burly owner and walked out.

Cold wind hit his face again. He checked the time in his watch. It was going to be eight. His mind automatically calculated India time.

'It must be around the same as here?' He thought. He walked back towards the apartments. His apartment was one of the most upmarket one in Times square called as, Helux.

It was recently renovated and located in New York city's highly sought-after hell's kitchen neighborhood. The Helux offered modern living spaces, Hudson River and city views, a fitness centre and basketball court as well as indoor and outdoor relaxation and entertainment areas.

Nilesh walked slowly towards the cluster of buildings. He decided to give one more try speaking to Sudha before retiring for that day. He did not want to try from his mobile as the number could be detected. He wanted a first-person information from her.

He was the world to her just six months back, just before he shifted to New York just before he got a job, just before they parted ways, just before she went back to India. How many just 'befores' were there now?

He walked past trudging through the accumulating snow on the foot path and calculating the just 'befores.' Only that his heart was aching so hard since, he heard the news that he wanted to make sure. He wanted to hear it from her.

He was not sure who would come on the line whether she would answer, if one of her parents would find out about him and bang the phone? Did they know about him at all? He was not sure. But still he wanted to speak to make sure. She owed it to him.

"Yes! She owes it! She cannot leave this way. I will find out in a minute, it is all a lie and come off laughing!" He told himself.

He wanted to try one more time before he gave up! From this booth, from some part of this world, from this unknown number. He wanted to be anonymous and speak, did not know why? When they were together, he was anonymous.
She had promised to talk to her folks about him. So now he was respecting that! Of course! When you

are with someone you respect their feelings. Don't you? Should he? He has to find out! "We exist or not!"

He told himself loud enough this time , to disperse a few bystanders.

He was not sure, but he wanted to make sure 'they' still existed. 'They' still, still existed. 'They' as in 'they!' He walked as the cold weather cut through his clothes. His eyes made tears that turned into icicles. He had no world other than 'they'. He had to find out. Now or never. If 'they' was still there! His heart pained and a tear threatening to roll down, only that the chill turned it into something else!

'If Sudha saw me this way, she would be so touched. She would just take me in her arms!'

His mind raced two and fro.

"My Parents are not very forthright about your Sindhi community." Sudha had rejoined once as Nilesh broached up the topic of their marriage. "My parents will have their reservations."

Nilesh nodded. They were in their final year of MBA at James Cook University Singapore. Nilesh was doing his master's in information technology computing and Networking while Sudha was studying Master's in International Tourism.

"Nilesh you must understand my parents will not allow me to be with you."
"I will try and win them over. Like Chetan Bhagat in two States?" He had joked.

In the heart of hearts, they both knew that it was impossible for both to please her parents. His parents came across as more open.

"Hmm. Still?" He had reflected long on what she was saying.

Both could not imagine their lives without each other.

Both had sat in front of the Merlion square holding each other. In warmth of their embrace they would dream their future.

Nilesh dodged a couple who walked past hand in hand. He looked over his shoulder at them. They were almost stuck together 'as one' shoulder to shoulder. How he missed Sudha. Such couples often made him feel most desperate to be in a relationship. He had no energy anymore to move ahead.

He wanted to wail but instead sat on the heightened cobbled side walk supporting himself with a lamp post on the side of the road. A homeless person was walking the street, singing loud as the rest of the pedestrians walked past him unheeding. He sat in the traffic rich street in the Times square and smoked as his mind was far away in Chandigarh. It's been six months and seemed like sixty long years since he spoke to her at length!

Was it difficult?

"Very." He uttered loud as a man passing leered. Scenes of people hanging around the square smoking or drinking from a can were very common. Nilesh walked unhurried.

A guitarist played at a distance to a small crowd that gathered to admire his resounding strings.
'This world is full of talent but only a few get the opportunity to show it.' He mused as he snubbed the cigarette on the mouth of the dustbin standing next to him.

He checked his watch that showed 8.20.

The time moved at a slow pace.

He wondered if he should call Sudha?

He slowly got up and walked to the booth. There was an old woman talking loudly to someone inside. He waited patiently. The talk was long, and the night was cold. The snow blanket seemed to be thickening by the hour. He pulled the long jacket close to him and shivered as he waited.

Sudha should be up by now. News had it that she was married. It was not clear whether she was getting married or already married.

'Should not be late before she talks to me!' Nilesh thought desperately. The news had just percolated in through one of his friends. He was at tether ends.

"Was she married already or was going to get married?" He again spoke to himself loudly. The passers glanced amused. He kicked a pebble and waited. Mind running riot.

"I will come home and speak to your parents." He had suggested and begged at the same time once she was prepared to leave Singapore. A couple of months were still remaining of his education. He had also got this job in New York!

"What is the problem? I am handsome, highly educated. Now I have a job in New York!"

"But they will not understand." Sudha retorted. "My parents are very orthodox south Indians. They believe in only our community marriages. Not in inter cast and all."

"What nonsense. Even today they think so?"

"Yep." Shockingly and in a weird way Sudha had never broached the topic, shrugged it off every time,in the two years they lived in together.

'She must be scared of her parents that's why!' He often mused.

"I tell you there is something fishy about this whole affair." His bosom pal Pawan had rejoined after Nilesh recounted his heart touching tale of romance and how his girlfriend was leaving for India.

"What are you saying?" Nilesh had almost screamed.

"I am heart-broken already, and you cannot speak like this."

"But I am not very sure about this girl. I was not from the beginning."

"Now shut up ok?"

"Ok." His friend had shrugged moving his head incredulous.
Then at the airport she was in tears.

"Sudha I am going to miss you." She was at the verge of getting into the departure queue.

She patted him on the back as he hugged her tight with the liquid in his eyes threatened to show which he wanted to save as an inappropriate commodity.
"I know but what to do?"

She was quiet for some time.

He had disentangled to plant a light kiss on her forehead to take her lips by storm next. Their chemistry was out of this world and that was the best part of their being together. As they disengaged after a whole 5-minute public kiss to the entertainment of other people, she had smiled looking up.

There was a strange light in her eyes.

She looked weak, powerless tears in her eyes shown like stars. He took both her palms in his to morph them with kisses like an insecure animal.

"Please allow me to come and speak to your parents."

"It's not going to work out!"

She spoke almost certainly. "You do not know my parents. They will never allow us to unite."

"How can you say that?" He almost added immediately. "Do you love me?"

He felt he saw a certain expression in her eyes. That moment she was a stranger again.

Nilesh pushed at an imaginary something under his foot. The lady was taking long. He took a long drawl at the ciggy. Instead of warm comfort the nicotine created snot and cough. His mind racing back to decipher that strange expression assessed.

'What was it? Resignation?'

"Yes!" The answer was almost immediate to the query of marriage to her. But he had felt a flicker of something missing there.

He hugged as a parting gift at the airport, while his friends warning 'There is something about this girl…' reverberated soundly.

He shrugged. They had the most wonderful two and a half years behind them. The chemistry was out of the world and he was madly in love with Sudha's brains too.

"You will call the moment you reach, won't you? You would be taking a flight again from Delhi?"

"To Chandigarh." She rejoined. She felt almost excited to him.

"Are you not unhappy that you are leaving me?" He added as a last desperate measure.

She nodded affirmative.

She needed to go by then. A long baggage queue was already lining up in the front.
She smiled ruefully, and he kissed her to endure the taste of her lips till they met again, before disengaging himself reluctantly.

He came to his senses as the booth door banged
and the lady walked out angry muttering under
her breath, some intangibles as she seemed to have
fought with someone on the other end. Nilesh
walked ahead in. He tried the same number several
times.

"Damn." He said to himself like a mad man.

"What the heck… I will go home and call," was his
final resolve as the winter night progressed gnawing
away his residual resolve.

He was no more bothered. The minutes tickled
slowly by. His decision dejected him as another
caller waited outside.

'Life is a bitch!' He snarled. The whole time it was
a self-dialogue that got to his anxious being further
in. Frustrated, fuming, again reasoning, anxious, he
reverted his steps to the apartment. His mind would
turn up and down, then down and up again like a
bi-polar imbecile.

En-way, he checked himself walking into a limo
as the angry driver waved him to move. This was
generally never the case during sane times. After
crossing he waited impatiently at the next road for
the signal to turn for pedestrian crossing.

He trudged with the crowd with a mind full of

Sudha! A couple of drunks moved past almost colliding into him this time.

He quickly tackled the next part of the road to his apartment. The cold was unbearable by now. The snow was steadily falling making a thin coat on people and by the time he entered the warmth of his room there was a film over his head and clothes.

He disengaged himself from the warm clothes laden with snow, hanging them on the side stand next to the door. He looked around the lonely room with hands on his hips till he decided to squat in front of the T.V skipping channels. Finally, he stopped to watch a movie. It was a beautiful fifties Gregory Peck romance.

His mind refused to focus. Most of the times Television played as distraction rather than a source of entertainment.

He looked on aimlessly and moved towards the kitchen. He poured Kingfisher from the can that he had bought at the Indian stores into a disposable plastic transparent glass.

Along with the left-out beer in the can he moved to the seating area and sat aimlessly in front of the idiot box.
Sudha's voice reverberated in his ears.

"Let's go movies. I love 50's slow romance and funny antics of lovers." She would often say.

Old movies in Singapore played only in a few theaters. His mind raced back.
It was a Saturday and they had just walked out of a Hindi movie Jism-2 Carnival theater Singapore, the house of Indian movies.

"I did not like Sunny Leone." laughed Sudha loud.
"Well I loved her!" Nilesh shrugged and he became the brunt of her mock punches. That very moment he had grabbed to kiss her hard in the middle of the exit itself, as amused people looked elsewhere. While crowd walked past, they kissed fervently, shameless in the middle of a theatre.

Now Nilesh sipped and sighed wondering if Sudha thought of all of their beautiful days. He poured the whole contents, into the glass, now he was a little groggy from alcohol, but the memory was sharp.

After the movie that day they had dinner at the Serangoon road 'Indian Curry' restaurant. It was one of their favorite hubs, that dished out south Indian food. They both had cherished it back then.

Nilesh took another sip of the alcohol at hand.

The love make afterwards was crystal clear in his mind too.
He smiled as he took another sip. His insides ached, and he felt horny that very moment. The longing in his heart grew. He stopped the temptation to call Sudha again. Instead he took another sip. As alcohol kicked in, his mind started racing on all probabilities.

On the hindsight he felt if she had saved his number. The last time he called, she had sounded very uncertain about whom she was talking to.

'Maybe, she was pretending?' He told himself.

Anyways she was very conspicuous by not calling him for long after reaching India. The gap of five days had felt endless. While he called her several times later, she sounded not enthusiastic either.

'It is the jet lag and the whole cultural change a person goes through when they reach home.' He would reason. The changed dynamics was a cause for worry so was pain.

When they were together, she could not live a single minute without him so this behavior was unfathomable.

'That is at least what she told me!' He took a long sip. The liquid cut through his insides mingled with pain that was searing through his being.

After those initial days he shifted to the U.S and the contacts changed too.
They had a slight gap of a few days when they had not spoken to each other again. They were insanely painful. He made the efforts to retain the magic though with frequent calls. His frantic calls went unanswered for days. Making him doubt the contact

number itself.

He could not get in touch for a while as his numbers changed after reaching the U.S again.

He took a sip once more. The movie seemed to play senselessly in front of his eyes. He skipped channels. Finally, settled for a show on Nat Geo. They were building beautiful homes. One after the other beautiful infra-structural wonders were being projected.

He sighed and gulped more alcohol.

Memories flooded. He swore. Everything seemed to remind of her. This was one of their favorite programs too during their dating period. Naturally, both dreamt of a beautiful home. His throat felt dry as a tear threatened to fall. He allowed it. As his face smothered with unending tears, he made no effort to brush them off. He drank the entire contents and looked on at the screen like an idiot. He felt vacant and aimless. That was the worst feeling of all. He dreaded slipping into that nothingness from time to time.

"We are going to make the best home in the world. I am going to decorate it with my own hands." Sudha would often say by nuzzling close to him after dinner.

They had made mad lovemaking after each Saturday movie session and Sundays golden dawn was the dawn to look forward to for them.

His eyes had a misty far-away look now! His mind played a zig saw puzzle. It went back to the memories of their meetings.

How they came together was also a story. Since they studied in the same university, they would cross the street eyeing each other.

A few days later they smiled as greeting. After some, they wished the time of the day. One of those crossings started the conversations- The same ethnicity, helped in bonding.

Their address in Singapore was WILBY CENTRAL-15 Queen Street. Both lived close by in serviced apartments that they realized after many, many meetings.

"I am from Chandigarh." Was the first sentence that Sudha had uttered.

"I am from Delhi."
"Oh."

"I am doing my IT engineering." Nilesh had prompted.

"I am into Master's in International Tourism."

"Wow! That is a great field too."

"It's good as I want to establish my own business in the long run."

"Do you want to settle abroad?" He had asked.

"No in Chandigarh. I love that place and my parents are settled there too."
Came her quick reply.

"If you get married to someone… then?" He had pressed on. In a very familiar Indian way. "You will have to shift right?"

She kept mum. After that conversation they fell silent and went their different ways for the day.

His jigsaw puzzle mind reasoned. Was she sure then? Did she really want a marriage with him?

As the alcohol ran down his throat his doubts made the tears back in his eyes.

'Was she sure then?'

He saw the time. It was 9.40 and he was sure that the Sun must be burning the city of Chandigarh. She must not have saved his number otherwise would not she be calling him? Besides this was a new contact. So why was he so touchy about she calling or he calling? His trepidation was all for her folks finding out about them and torturing his Sudha.

He asserted to himself like a lunatic. The effect of alcohol was taking over him.

"I will call you. Please do not call." She had pleaded.

"My parents might find out!" She had begged.

"So? I am ready to marry you! Ready to come and talk to them!"

"No, no, no … you do not understand."

"What?"

"There is a time for everything!" She had cut the call. Most of her calls were from public booths and he obviously did not save them as they were of no use.

He was so far. He felt so very drawn away- Helpless.

His thoughts went back to his Singapore days. He tried her number after shrugging away his fears that someone could detect it. It was now or never.

'I am so far. I have nothing to lose.'

'But what about Sudha? I will tell her to fake it as

someone else. A friend maybe? But that is if she takes it. Why is she not taking it?'

He tried again. But again! He got no response. He tried again. Yet nothing.

After a while he poured the entire can and took several sips. He could feel the beer have an effect on his senses by now deeply.

'I will try one more time.'

He decided. He called. After 7 to 8 rings the call was answered. It was a man.

Nilesh was taken aback and was worried that it could be a male member from the family. He immediately reacted.

"May I speak with Sudha?"

"Who is this?" The male asked.

Nilesh thought quickly.

"I am calling from New York."

"Yes?"

"I wanted to know if she would be interested to do a Doctoral thesis in Client management?" It was a wild sentence, he threw. If the man was intelligent, he would know that it would be night in the New York city and no university office functioned that late. Nilesh thought quickly.

"This is the PR agency call centre of the New York University. We get the numbers of students from all over the world, so we make calls in different parts of the globe day and night. I am an Indian student myself and work here at the centre."

He added and found himself going red in the face at his own invent. He waited with bated breath as the man at the mobile called out to Sudha.

"Sudhi…"

'Sudhi?' Must be her papa.' Nilesh wondered if the marriage was taking place at home and all the people were there or she was alone, and someone happened to pick the call?

The alcohol made him dizzy. The situation was not helping either.
His wait seemed endless.

Since it was morning time the place seemed noiseless. The background was peaceful.

After a while somebody came in as he heard the hustle at the other end.

"It's someone from New York University. Do you want to take the call?"

"New York? Hmm. What will I do now?" It was Sudha.

"Talk to them then? Refuse?" said the man.

He seemed to speak in a matter of fact tone and it was Sudha on the line after a while.

"Hi?"

"Hi… It's me Sudha…!" Nilesh's heart pounded with excitement on hearing her voice.

On the other side there was a quiet moment.

"I won't be interested to study further…"

"Sudha it's me… Nilesh!" Nilesh's heart was in his mouth.

"I told you, I won't be interested to study further."

"Sudha, sweetheart. It's me. If you don't want, don't talk just say yes or no. Are you getting married?"

"No! As I said I am not interested."

"Who is it?' The man on the other side seemed to

have entered the room.

"Who is it?" Again, the guy enquired sounding a bit agitated.

"The same guy as you had spoken to. He is enquiring if I am interested to join the advanced courses in Hospitality." Sudha explained. Her voice seemed to falter a bit.

"Ok. Do you?" The man's voice sounded from a distance.

Nilesh was restless on his side. Strangely, a shaft of jealousy ran through his spine on envisioning a man so close to Sudha. He found his voice finally through his alcohol laden brains to speak.

"Sudha it's me!!! Nilesh!" He tried desperately.

"I know but I am not interested." She almost seemed to giggle into the line. Or was he imagining?

"Tell me are you getting married?"

"What? Noooooo! I am not interested right now. I will let you know if I am."

"I know that someone is in the room with you, who should not listen to this."
Nilesh added desperately. "But let me know in yes

or no when I ask you."

"Ok!"

"Are you getting married? Why? To whom? Is it true?"

"When?" was all that she asked.

"Right now!"

"Who told you that?"

"I came to know?"

"Who is it?" The man thundered from afar.

Again, there was a long pause and the line went dead.

Nilesh looked at the instrument for a while and for a long time Sudha's voice reverberated in his ears. His facial muscles were twitching with nervousness and excitement had made him numb. The thrill of listening to her was so awesome but he was where he had started.

Her voice that he could hear after such a long time was music. Should he just leave with what he heard from her or should he just sit there and console himself? He was at a loss of thoughts. The alcohol was making him feel like a Zombie. He stood gingerly and went into the toilet. He sat on the seat long, letting out the liquids and finding no out let for thoughts of Sudha though.

Her voice echoed constantly.

"No, No! No! Not interested!"

He wanted to let out anger, frustration, hatred, everything together. All the demonic emotions gripped his core. Who was the man? What was he doing there? He sounded young!

That question he avoided though he could not think straight. Why should she listen to him? Did not he have the right to know? Did not he need to know? Was not it her duty to tell?

'What duty?' he asked himself as a rebound to his own doubt. As a mad man talking to himself about the answerless questions, he wanted to cave into a fetal position and die. Instead he got up with wobbly legs into the bedroom. The disposal of the liquids from his body seemed to make it lighter and his head clearer.

He had no answers but wanted all.

How was he going to know what was happening in her life? He racked his brains.

He decided to finally call the guy who gave him the news and he dialed his number.

The phone rang several times with no answer.

Sudha seemed close to the man in the room. Could be her father or a cousin?' He reasoned. 'He does not sound like her father though. Does not sound old!' He answered himself.

Brushing the negative thoughts, he sat with his head in his hands for clarity.

'He seems to be youthful from his voice! Could be a cousin. Yes, yes a cousin!' he decided!

'I cannot do anything sitting here. I have to find the truth though.' He wondered.

Lately she was not calling him at all. As they had parted ways the onus of the responsibility of calling him was on her as she had warned him against her folks finding out about them. She had never kept that promise. He was the one who ceaselessly persuaded her by getting in touch.

His empty bowls burned. He continued nevertheless, he called the number again. There was no answer.

'Was it some prank? Could be possible. Was Sudha happy to take my call? She must be?'

The short conversation with her went on in his head like a recorder till he felt, he would go crazy. His pounding heart had rested but his brain refused peace playing havoc by creating stories. Questions floated in and out. He needed to find out. But how? He was stuck with the man's voice, sudden suspenseful silence from her, at his questions.

'Errh' he wanted to pull his hair. Instead, he wobbled to the kitchen and brought out a new can of liquid liquor to put his mind at ease.

He walked over to the bedroom with the drink that refused to give respite somehow. It was nearly midnight now. He looked aimlessly for a while and finally pulled over the comforter to the seating area. Sleeping alone on that huge bed made him feel mad. He switched off the lights except for the one in the corners, clicked on the T.V., coiled on the sofa watching the romantic escapades of the 50s that garnered no attention.

He gathered himself, as close as possible, slept in a fetus position with tears running down like an infant. The beer cans, plastic glasses with an active T.V set, he looked somewhat like a homeless man.

He woke up to the noise of television and a couple romancing on the screen at midnight. He switched it off and pulled himself close. Clutching his knees together to his throat as near as possible he went into the oblivion of darkness that seemed unending. Coiled deeper into the covers he wanted to become invisible. After a while the darkness dispersed. There standing was his beloved Sudha.

Yes! There she was. Now she was not speaking monosyllables but was making love to his parched body.

He woke the next day feeling groggy with a splitting head. As the realization seeped in, the muddy feelings threatened to take hold again. He just wanted nothing but to coil back in. His eyes refused to open and see. What they will anyway? He thought.

That day was a Sunday. The day seemed to span, endlessly as he made to spread his long-coiled limbs on the narrow mattress. So, as he woke to the realization that there was nothing to look forward to. He checked his mobile the only bridge to the outside world. He was surprised to find, as to how many calls he had made to the same number unintelligibly in his drunkenness. There was no response of course!

The Sunday crawled by. He finished all the tasks required to be done. Done; but his mind refused to forget her.

When the lights were out, and he spread on the bed that night with his laptop in his lap he went to his

fb account.   Anything and everything to distract himself. Next involuntarily, he sauntered to find Sudha's account. He cursed himself for it. But he did anyway. With super human strength he was done with the day. Now there was no escaping his own devil of a mind.
He could not find it. He checked and double checked. Tried several combinations of names.

'Did she remove her profile?' He wondered. 'Or, am I on the right name?'

He knew that as a fact she never 'show cased' him in public as her boyfriend. That was also the most downside of their whole dating scenario.

He sighed.

'How could not I see the red flags?'

Why was she so social media shy? She was one person who had an account from her school days on fb, but never uploaded many pictures.

He would spy on her with the intention of finding an old crush. His profile remained private on her account. He never ever found their pictures in her friends list. That made him very angry sometimes but had allowed to pass by, for the love of her.
She would say, she was very scared of her parents, so she was not posting their pics. All said and done

he felt somehow cheated for not being introduced as her boyfriend.

She would retaliate:

"I am a very private person and do not want to go public about anything."

Her fb account had hardly ten pictures and most of them were from her school with her batch mates.

He went back to his account to check on his friends and to find what was happening. He skipped through several and his gaze fell on Manisha's. She happened to be one of their common friends. He conversed with her sometimes on the social media, just commenting or replying to her posts.

Again, his mind went back to Sudha. He wanted to hit his head against a brick wall. But then there was no curing him. He had totally forgotten that Manisha even existed till that moment. His heart raced, and his hopes went up as he scrolled through the account. She had posted several pictures. They were interesting, and he got lost in them for a while. Looking at the heavily loaded pictures with a man, he realized,

'Maybe, she has tied the knot recently.'

The pictures were from different parts of the country;

from North and South of India.

In some pictures, there were a lot of people in formal attires of all ages as well.

'Must be her extended family!' He observed.

While going through one of the pictures in the series of mobile uploads, he stopped short.

'Was she? Was she not?'

'She must have gone to meet her friend? The convenience of staying in the same city of course!' He reasoned grudgingly.

They were party pictures of a social gathering in which she was visible. Then on, his eyes ran hungrily on the upload.

'Wait! Who was next to her?'

In most pictures, Sudha was not visible except for her face and a portion of her body next to Manisha.

'Oh Shit! Who is this guy? He is standing so close to her?' Nilesh's eyes widened, while his heart cart-wheeled.

'Wait both were holding hands too!' Nilesh froze! The picture in itself was a beautiful one with his 'lady love' looking deep into the other man's eyes.

A slow flow of perspiration made its way from the corner of his ear to the nape of his neck.

'Is he a friend?'

He looked closer. His hands twitched while his brow dripped in spite of the -7 degrees temperature. He swiped his forehead in an involuntary action with the back of his hand. He took in more details.

Sudha's back was reclining on to the guy's chest as if to support her. He was holding her hand too.

He had not had an anxiety attack in a long time from Singapore student days. He double checked dates. They were all very recent. A stab of deceit forked through him.

'Was he her fiancé?' He wanted to believe the negative but, but…

He checked Manisha's account details for her contact. He was disappointed.
'Who put numbers on fb?'

He questioned his own stupidity.

As his hands and feet started to twitch and body convulsed, he shut his eyes.

Nilesh's heart was pounding in a super-sonic speed in his mouth. Clammy fingers refused a hold on the machine buttons.

'Who were our common friends?' He tried to think sane through it all surprising himself.

As soon as his fingers could function, he went through several accounts to narrow in on a common friend's number. He dialed it with no luck.
'It is a Monday morning Goddamn, and the people might be preparing to go to work. While I try to figure out my girlfriends love status!'

He hated himself. But he was a victim of his predicament. Here he was on a cold chilling winter night in New York feeling terribly lonely stalking his girl who might be not his anymore! He wished no such fate even to his worst enemies.

'It's a bad place to be!' He cursed. He wanted to snivel!

He went back to Manisha's account in desperation. As the devil would have it, he found a couple of more pictures of Sudha with the guy hand in hand. The hands were entwined, they seemed very close, Sudha had a knowing expression on her face.

The clam increased.
He dissected other details of proximity in the

uploads.

By now his face was twitching while the temples leaked. He shivered under the thick blankets. His heart almost felt outside his body.

He just put the laptop down and started whimpering. After a while the perspiration and tears became one, turned into cold water, threatening to flood the room, instead, turned into icicles.

He had forgotten to switch the heater on!

He cried alone. Here he was trying to contact his ex and there she was back home into the arms of another guy. He cried till his heart wrenched, threatened to shed from his chest.

'Wait! If he is her brother? A cousin? Possibly?' He again reasoned through the panic.

'Why jump to conclusions? How much do I know about her family?' Now he was talking to himself very loudly.

'One should not conclude till one is very sure about everything? Yes, yes all and everything.' He told himself.

He reasoned, he wept, he brushed aside thoughts, he reasoned, he wept. It continued. Bouts of reasoning and weeping till he fell into a restless sleep in a fetal position. On the large bed he fell on a fragment. He did not want to live anymore. Whole night he dreamt about her. About her in another man's arms. Another man making love to her. Another man, another man, another, another, another.

He woke up drenched in cold sweat several times! There was no escaping, images of Sudha with another man in close proximity, Sudha's back to him, Sudha from fb, Sudha laughing into his face haunted his wakeful state! Sudha! Sudha! Sudha! To fall into a nightmarish sleep again.

As the dawn advanced, he woke up exhausted to a new painful day.
The thought paramount was what if, what if she was married or what if she was not?

He just willed himself to shut his brains and wait till the next time he could contact her. He finally made peace.

But where was she? She was not even taking his calls nor was she calling him? How was he going to decide? How would he call her or contact her?

The next day was office day. The dreaded day in the frame of mind that he was!

He had to identify priorities based on the milestones set by the clients. He was working on projects to meet deadlines by providing team leadership.

How was he to do all that in a shit state of mind? Numbers and milestones jumbled in front of his vision.

He had a couple of meetings from identifying the selling opportunities. They seemed like huge boulders. His mind was not in the right place!

Mark was his boss and by midday, he wanted to have a word with him. He asked Nilesh to take a seat.

"Management was always looking for ways to improve service and make more money. Inspiring co-workers, everyone around to motivate them towards excellence. We find you to be that person who is motivating and always inspiring others to excel. Well, done Nilesh!"

'Oh ya?' He thought. This work no more gave him exhilaration. He was almost absent in the room though physically present.
Nilesh nodded in stupor. How could he react positive as all he cared was a woman called Sudha?

"Do you have your family here?" His boss was asking.
Nilesh swung his head from side to side. The habit that was so Indian and most Americans found it very amusing.

"No, not yet married."

"Oh! Hope to see you married soon. A girlfriend?" The boss asked.

'Oh no. Not here too!' He swung his head.

"No, I mean yes?" He added quickly.

Mark looked confused.

"I mean, I have one, but she is in India right now!" Nilesh clarified quickly.

"It's complicated." Nilesh finally summed.

"I understand, I understand. Complicated is not good." Mark moved in his chair so did his middle-aged pot belly.

"It's not a good place to be in! Is it?"

Nilesh shrugged though he was not feeling nonchalant. He took leave of Mark on that.

After finishing his pending details on the deadlines and project plans, Nilesh decided to leave for the day!

Most New-Yorkers packed food home. He drove into a Mac and picked a burger.

He drove back.

After a brief hot shower and getting into his pajamas he sauntered in his night clothes with the burger in hand. He switched on the T.V. It made random sounds in the back ground as he finished dinner.

Unable to concentrate he switched it off. He sat there on the carpet looking vacantly out of the window at the Christmas lights. Some houses looked beautiful!

With the gifts on the trees and the children playing around it was a merry family time. He walked towards the French windows, the only beautiful feature about his house. He could see a couple of families around the tables having their supper and chatting away excitedly in the opposite building. He missed his parents, siblings and warmth of his home back in India. He remembered the festive times when the entire family celebrated Diwali.

The person at the back of his mind creeped in. Eyes misted.

Sudha was very clear that she wanted to settle in India. There were no two ways about it. She could not for the life of her miss out on the beautiful family times and festivals. She was ready to bear with the pain of visiting relatives, gossiping neighbors to a life of solitude in New York or anywhere in the world.

'I wanted to settle here!' He looked at his reflection, in the window pane. For some reason, he could not recognize himself.

He screamed silently. The only way to compensate that, he dialed her number several times like a mad man. He went on and on and on for some time, hundreds of times. No luck!

Anger filled him. The indisputable feeling of vacant came back!

'Oh! God how she creeps into me?' he cursed himself. His fingers fumbled with the dial pad.

'She is mine. She belongs to me. Without a doubt. Why should not I call then? She is all over my soul!'

Angry but undecided, he walked to his refrigerator and drank the entire bottle of alcohol within minutes.

He finally pressed the number he was tracing with his fingers. No answer. He tried again, again, again and again.

Frustrated he just threw the instrument. It found it's place in the corner in its hurled momentum. Frustrated, angry and alone he just slumped on the bed that night.

That night, his dreams were full of the lady who

made him mad. He dreamt of trying to reach her without avail.

His troubled sleep was wrought with unsuccessful attempts to contact her. He tossed and turned till the images blurred and the hapless feelings of loss rode over his body with intense sweat.

Finally, finally he accomplished. He got through. The phone rang at the other end. In the improvised nightmare situation elation took over. Anxiety and hope mingled. Feelings of relief ensued.

'Only that there was something wrong with the sound at the other end. Seriously? What? What was it? It was too shrill and too loud too weirdly close it was almost in his ear!'

Now the relief jumbled to become confusion and thoughts conglomerated to fight.
It was too much to handle for one dream! Dream became reality as he woke up to the insistent sound of his mobile ringing.

Now the reality was nightmare as he crawled on his fours, in a sleepy stupor in the darkness of his home feeling the corners for the instrument. The escaping street light made the active mobile visible after a while of crawling and groping.

His sleep laced voice could somehow manage a tentative- "Hello?"

"Hellooooo??" He repeated.

"Hello!" came a familiar voice.

He sat up.

"Sudha?"

"Hmmm! Don't you understand that you should not call?"

"What... the? What? What the? What do you mean? I should not call?"

"Don't you know that I don't want to be in touch?"

By now he squeezed his eyes willing them to open, trying to be fully awake!
"You, you don't want to be in touch? But...?"

"Yes! Don't call me."

"Are you married now?" The question wobbled out. The one he wanted to ask in his nightmares.

"I was always a married woman!"

He just sat there registering the sounds that made

those dreaded expressions.   The syllables, that shrunk him to half a size.

"What? I don't understand!" He managed at last.

By now sleep and grogginess gave way to a forbidding feeling of lack. In a strange way the carpet under him seemed to slip away! His whole world turned into a crazy frenzy.

"You were married means what?" He managed with a froth-filled mouth that is experienced only in intense over whelm of pain.

"I was always married Nilesh. I was married even when I was with you in Singapore! Only that I did not tell you!"

"You mean? You mean?"

"I needed support and someone to lean on in a foreign land. To wade off loneliness you can say. You seemed too gullible and forth coming. So I took you!" she almost laughed.

"Oh! Come on! Don't be such a prude! You certainly know the term-Friends with benefits?"

"Took you?" He managed somehow to ask. The froth went in and out mingled with warm tears.

He was a scape goat of some fancy Hollywood

movie called Friends with benefits? Only that this fu@#$%* & life was not, not, not that movie!

"You mean all the time you were… cheating? All the time you were playing with me? Now you just call to tell me this? This, This? Now! You don't want to talk? Now you are telling me this, this shit with a wide smile on your face? I need an explanation! I, I need it! You cannot, cannot...... you, you, you!"

There was utter silence on the other end simply because the call was not on!

As the cold night turned colder and the streets fell more silent, the room caved in on him. He coiled and coiled till there was none left!

.

Ribs ached as his heart throbbed painfully exerting to exist inside him. A feeling of utter hopelessness and desertion came and went in waves!
'I don't know what is more painful; the pain of deception or the pain of separation?' The love of his life Sudha was a cheating, conniving bag of lies?
The thought of his parents stopped him from doing something drastic.

The next day he woke up in the corner from where his life ended, in a fetal position, realizing that he had to go on. His head full of searing pain transmitted ache to his eyes. Alcohol, deception and gloom took over the promise of a new day.

The days just passed in a haze. Months happened to him. His longing for Sudha turned into an involuntary pain filled with hatred. Believing in women was no more easy.

He worked his days at the office desk, he spent the nights coiled into a ball on the bed. He lived because he could breath. He lived because he lived.

Where his heart was there was a lump now. It did its job, but it had turned into a black heavy stone. He was unaware that the poison crept into the inner recesses till it poured out to afflict even the simple cycles of his existence. He ate less, spoke less, slept less, groomed less. Less of everything captured his vision too. Only he did not realize that one lived fully or did not! One did not abuse alcohol as a solution.

The self-destructive journey killed his vital surviving energy and within months he was discovered in his cubicle by a good friend in a semi unconscious state.

Thanks to the kind-hearted gentleman and his family he was nurtured back to health on time. His friends asked him to see a therapist and he did.

After Two years----

Nilesh realized very early on during therapy that

alcohol was not a solution to anyone's problems. This knowledge helped him see through the difficult phase.

Today he is helping others walk the difficult path to recovery.

He works today with a men's organization in New York that counsels abused men of all types. They include men having relationship issues, issues concerning faith, trust, anger management, trauma, family of origin issues, sex addiction, domestic abuse, drug and alcohol abuse.

The organization works towards ensuring the core healing of body, mind and spirit to promote larger feelings of goodness.

He plans to spread the message around the globe by focusing on a balance of energy flow, to heal the body and for a drug-free life.

❊ ❊ ❊